DACHSHUND TAILS RESCUED

And Other Tales

by Marilyn Cochran Mosley

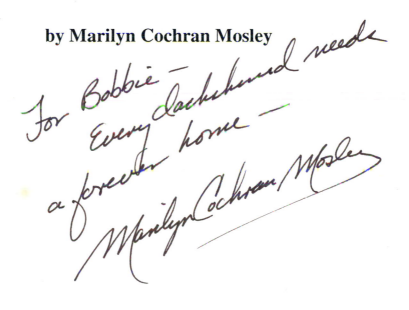

For Bobbie —
Every dachshund needs
a forever home —

Marilyn Cochran Mosley

Cover art by Sueellen Ross

Printed in Victoria, Canada

National Library of Canada Cataloguing in Publication Data

Mosley, Marilyn Cochran, 1938-
　　　Dachsund tails rescued and other tales / Marilyn
Cochran Mosley.
ISBN 1-55395-562-5
I. Title.
PS3613.O774D33 2003　　　　　　813'.6　　　C2003-900137-7

TRAFFORD

This book was published *on-demand* in cooperation with Trafford Publishing.
On-demand publishing is a unique process and service of making a book available for retail sale to the public taking advantage of on-demand manufacturing and Internet marketing. **On-demand publishing** includes promotions, retail sales, manufacturing, order fulfilment, accounting and collecting royalties on behalf of the author.

Suite 6E, 2333 Government St., Victoria, B.C. V8T 4P4, CANADA
Phone　　　250-383-6864　　　Toll-free　　1-888-232-4444 (Canada & US)
Fax　　　　250-383-6804　　　E-mail　　　sales@trafford.com
Web site　　www.trafford.com　　TRAFFORD PUBLISHING IS A DIVISION OF TRAFFORD
HOLDINGS LTD.
Trafford Catalogue #02-1278　　　www.trafford.com/robots/02-1278.html

10　　　9　　　8　　　7　　　6　　　5

A special note of appreciation goes to Mary Anne "Zak" Thomas of Hoover, Alabama, and her long-haired dachshund, Benz Wolfgang Thomas, for encouraging Schultz and me to start and finish this book.

Thanks also go to Sally Larkin of Davis, California, Marian Brischle of San Francisco, California, and Diane Weber of Birmingham, Alabama, for their helpful comments, and to my wordsmith editor Virginia Harding of Rocklin, California.

Finally, a very special thank you to all of the individuals who contributed dachshund rescue stories for this book:

Roelie Carsouw
Kathy Crean
Bertha C. Hague
Mary Landers Horton
Shirley Jacobsen
Andy Kassier
Carol Kuechle
Maggie Rosenbaum
Mary Anne "Zak" Thomas
Scott West

Other books by Marilyn Cochran Mosley:

Dachshund Tails North
Dachshund Tails Up The Inside Passage
Dachshund Tails Down The Yukon

Alaskan Ferry Tales for Children (editor)

Dachshund Tails Rescued
And Other Tales

For Joyce Watford Delbridge, a very special lady who has been a writing mentor to me for many years,

and as a tribute to all of the dachshunds whose stories appear below.

Schultzie

TABLE OF CONTENTS

"People think that a dachshund is just a sort of short-legged, long-bodied dog. They do no realize that there are dogs … and then there are dachshunds. Dogs like to please their owners by doing what they are told. Dachshunds like to please themselves."

Dick King, <u>Smith's Animal Friends</u>, p. 54.

Prologue

Schultz is the teller of this story, for it's mostly his. But first, I will tell you about Schultzie.

Everyday is a new adventure for Schultz, whether he's home on Vashon Island in Puget Sound, Washington state or sniffing the air while traveling in the car along some highway. Stubbornness, playfulness and a talent for mischief are part of his personality, the thread of his story. Schultz's tale is about his coming to Vashon Island, finding his new family there, and meeting his pet primate, Marilyn. Eiger, another rescue dachshund, joins him at the end of his tale.

Midway through the book Schultz introduces you to some of his favorite rescued friends.

The saga of Schultzie rescued kindled an interest in other dachsies needing a forever or permanent home.

Schultz had a home, and a good home, but his people were unable to keep him when he couldn't be toilet trained. I took him in to join my remaining four dachshunds that you can read about in my book, *Dachshund Tails Down The Yukon,* and the adventures they had as puppies. By the time Schultzie arrived they were senior citizens, and I found myself having to move from my home on the beach when my husband passed away. I had lived there for twenty-two years. Adding a year-and-a-half-old dachsie was a bit of a challenge. Schultzie adapted well.

Rescued dachshunds come from various situations ... displaced by the death of their owner, a divorce, a new baby, or a move to a place that won't accept animals. Some new owners find they are unprepared for the lifestyle requirements that exist when one takes on a dachshund. Other dachshunds, found as strays, find their way into rescue programs through local animal shelters. Some dachshunds are rescued from intolerable situations, such as Fritz was in Chapter 17. Thanks to volunteers, those dachshunds are retrieved from shelters before they are euthanasized and are kept in foster care until a forever home can be found. Others come from puppy mills, a deplorable situation, such as Scooter Pie's in Chapter 16.

Think of the rescue programs as a match-making service for dachshunds in need. As much information as possible is learned about the dog, then the search for an interested family begins.

Rescued dachshunds are not free. Expenses multiply as the dogs are nursed back to good health, ridding them of fleas, lice and ticks as well as internal parasites. Additional costs include spaying or neutering, cleaning teeth, clearing up skin problems, adjusting a dog's weight up or down, giving injections, feeding and housing until the right new home comes along.

There isn't a set adoption fee, as each dachshund has a different background. They are checked by a veterinarian, brought up-to-date on their shots, and spayed/neutered before placement. Some groups ask for a donation to cover the funds used for medical care and to help keep the group going; others have minimum adoption fees.

People need to remember that rescues, however, are not coins that fit in a slot, ka-ching. These dogs have gone through many different life experiences. Sometimes it is very difficult or impossible for a dachsie to adjust properly to one certain home or situation, new people, or other pets. Sometimes it is necessary to move them to another home, where some will do just fine. Unfortunately, others never make a successful transition.

Adopting a rescue dachshund can be more difficult than adopting a child. There's paperwork to fill out, questions to answer, and then prospective homes are checked to see if what was claimed is indeed true. But in the end, those rescued know they were saved and reward their new family with undying loyalty.

All of today's dachshunds, like Schultz, descended from hunting dogs living long ago in Western and Central

Europe. When burrowing under fences, in gardens or in beds of clean laundry, dachsies are merely continuing a heritage from their ancestors.

The dachsie's characteristic low and long body form is ideally suited for work both underground, and tracking through underbrush. Their ability to go both forward and backward in a crouching position, combined with their sturdy bodies and strong jaws, allows them to excel at bringing badger, fox or rabbit from their dens.

Dachshunds are long-standing members of the Dog World, with evidence that dogs of dachshund type were known in ancient times. The dachsie family tree used today dates back to the fifteenth century, to the training of badger hounds bred by German foresters. The breed was well established by the late 1800s. German pedigrees are recorded as far back as 1859. In the United States, between 1879 and 1885, only eleven dachshunds were registered.

Dachshunds were initially introduced into North America about 1880, and gained popularity, until the world wars. Then, because of their German origin, they suffered a setback. Since then, due to the efforts of dedicated breeders, they have regained their status as one of our best-known and most popular breeds.

Dach, means "badger" in German; *hund* means "dog." The two words are put together and pronounced as one— "doxhoont." Hence the name of these courageous little dogs, shaped long and low, who have the courage, skill, and build to track badgers into their burrows.

Dachshunds are exceedingly stubborn. And a good thing! As the smallest breed used for hunting, they need all their pluck and intelligence to do their job and survive, just as important, to help them circumvent anything they choose *not* to do—like be prudent. That's a problem that often propels dachsies into trouble. They are courageous to the point of rashness.

Both smooth-hair and long-hair dachshunds have existed since the origins of the breed. The wirehaired dachshund appears to have been developed later, possibly by the introduction of some wire-hair terrier-type blood.

Chapter 1

A New Home

My name is Schultz, actually Schultz Junior, after my dad. I belong to that canine group known as *dachshunds.* This automatically gives me the reputation of being outstandingly stubborn, so much so that I lost my first home. When my masters tried to convince me to pee outside, I'd ignore them, walk right into the house and lift my leg. They weren't bad people, they just didn't understand a little dog like me, and didn't know what to do with me. But right now, let's get on with my tail, I mean tale.

Smell was my first memory, and Heidi, that's my mom, always smelled good. Her scent was a bouquet of fresh warm milk, protection and love. When my eyes finally opened about a week after I was born, I saw that she was a beautiful raven black. There were brown splashes of fur above her eyes that moved up and down when she laughed. Matching brown spots above each toe completed her couture.

Her whiskers tickled when she licked me. I wiggled all over and nuzzled right up against her belly.

What's this? Another dachshund? There. Right where I wanted to be, suckling, and slurping up enough dinner for three. Warm liquid spilled from the sides of her mouth. Her tummy bulged as if it were going to pop at any moment.

A small noise erupted from deep inside me. My sister didn't even look up, just tightened her hold on that teat and continued her engorgement, but mom heard. She nudged me gently but firmly to her other side.

Unlike mom, my sister was brown all over. Pudgy was an understatement. I glanced down at my own paws. They were brown, just like my sister's, not black at all. We were both short haired and smooth, but then so was mom. No long hairs, and no wires.

The emptiness in my stomach overcame all other thoughts. I grabbed the nipple in front of me with my whole mouth and began suckling for all I was worth. I didn't want my little piggy of a sister to get ahead of me. She soon collapsed in a heap, tiny beads of milk spilling out of her mouth and nose. I tumbled over and crashed right on top of her head. She was already asleep, and so was I—before you could say Schultz.

When I woke, mom was right there. So was my sister. She had wiggled up to another pap. I scrambled right beside her. The two of us drank until we could hold no more. Afterward, play, roll around, bite, growl. Then another heap! Sleep followed.

Mom's soft pink tongue kept us clean. During these grooming sessions she told us stories about dad. She always ended by telling us he looked just like we did, being brown all over from nose to tail, and then she would add that he was very handsome.

I tried to imagine a grown-up dachshund, all brown, and had a hard time doing it. After all, mom was black and that's what big dachshunds looked like. Also, little dachshunds had short noses.

Then one day dad showed up. His nose was even longer than mom's, but it was brown all over, except for

2

the black button he had at the end. He didn't want a thing to do with either me or my sister. He dashed from the room as if some dachshund demon were chasing him. Me! An apparition. I was only one-month old.

Marilyn, Schultz's human mistress, brought dad over because she wanted to see us, and, I guess, have him meet his offspring.

Now Marilyn, unlike dad, couldn't get close enough. She held us. She hugged us. She squeezed us, rolled us on our backs, tickling us both. We still smelled puppy, and Marilyn took in our scent. But since there were only two of us and Marilyn had other dachshunds, she wasn't going to keep either of us. We already had homes.

She sat right on the floor and played. I was bashful and tried to hide. My sister, much more forward, snuggled into her lap, then curled in a ball, dachshund fashion, and licked her fingers. Both of us were chubby and awkward.

During all the "oohing and awing," mom wouldn't come near us. In fact she growled, first at dad and then Marilyn. Her mistress put her into a back room. I guess mom thought one or both of them were going to eat us up or something. Exhausted when Marilyn left, we dropped in a pile of tails and feet, fat puppy flesh and fur.

Mom shot right over the moment Schultz and Marilyn went out the door. First she examined me, than my sister. She had been trying to wean us. Our teeth had developed into needle-sharp points. This time she sat, letting us have our fill, licking and nudging and making little loving sounds the whole time. Little did I know then that my dad Schultz and Marilyn were to become my family, but that was a whole year-and-a-half later.

Lots of fun things happened during my first year, even though I was separated from my sister and mom most of the time. I saw them occasionally, and more and more as time passed. My new human family and my mom's human family were related. My sister stayed with our mom.

But at my new home, trouble began to find me. At first it wasn't a big deal. I just didn't want to pee when my family thought I should. Potty training wasn't in the cards. Oh, I understood all right, but I had my own agenda. I didn't want to be bothered. Go outside when it was warm and comfortable indoors? No way! And when it rained? Forget it!

Nothing worked.

I was particularly bad when they left me home alone. I didn't like that at all and figured out a good way to punish them for their negligence. I left little calling cards as a reminder so they wouldn't do it again. This went on for more than a year, and by that time I was full grown and should have been trying to do better.

I ended up with my mom and sister all the time. But they couldn't keep three dachshunds, particularly one little bad boy who peed and pooped whenever and wherever he felt like it.

One day, amid tears and hurried words, I found myself on a ferry with my blue teddy bear, my white lamb's wool blanket, my water bowl, and my two favorite humans. They were crying, and hugging me, and crying more. It was a wet ferry crossing.

When we reached the other side, Marilyn greeted us. They handed me over to her, along with my blanket, my bowl and my teddy bear and ran for the ferry just as it was ready to pull out. I growled, puzzled, wondering why Marilyn showed up. She snuggled me up into her arms, and that was the last I ever saw of my first human family.

Well, Marilyn lived in a big house on the beach all by herself, as her husband had died. She sat down on the patio with me in tow. Then a great big bruiser of a dachshund jumped up into her lap squishing me almost flat. I realized then she didn't live by herself at all.

My gosh! It was my dad, and he had gained weight.

4

Twelve more feet jumped up to join him. Growls followed but soon quieted. Everyone looked like my dad, and all had a familiar smell. I guess it was a family resemblance. I had uncles. There was Moose. He bit my tail. I yelped. Can you imagine having an Uncle Moose? He was the smallest of all of them. I think Marilyn goofed when she named him.

Uncle Moose

Then there were Baron and MacDuff, better known as Duff. Baron was named, somewhat like the renowned beagle, for Baron von Richthofen, famed World War I ace fighter pilot. Because he flew a tri-plane, painted blood red, von Richthofen was dubbed "The Red Baron." Uncle Baron always wore a red collar. Baron was so easy-going he just would roll over when there was a scrap. Duff, on the other hand, was usually the instigator of those altercations.

They sniffed and nudged and sniffed me again. At first I was terrified as each one checked me out. Marilyn held me close and kept a protective arm around me. They soon lost interest, ignored me, and resumed their naps on the patio's warm cement.

Since my first family had named me after my dad, Marilyn had no choice. So Schultz, Junior it was. And when she called "Schultz," both my dad and I came running. Ha! Sometimes we did. More often it was time to hide in the bushes, overlook her pleas, or chase a cat or two. And Marilyn always had cats around.

On my first day exploring my new home, I discovered an in-and-out door. It was made especially for dachshunds. Wow!

I sniffed, my nose twitching. *Hmmmmmm.* Now what was this?

I stopped short.

A gray-striped cat walked right through the swinging door.

Meow! The air exploded with her odor. Her eyes became big as dinner plates. There was a moment's hesitation, a barely audible hiss. Then she continued unhurriedly on her way, daring me to interfere. Those pale blue eyes of hers, I suspected, could spew fire if she were so inclined.

Tasha was old and wise—a gray lynx-striped cat with "Siamese if you please" somewhere in her background. Marilyn had rescued her many years earlier from the Humane Society in Ketchikan. Tasha just

6

didn't chase, so she wasn't much fun. Later, when I got to know her better I liked to wrestle around with her, and when she became irritated with it all, her ears flattened out and a hissing sound erupted. That meant stop. I didn't push it. I stopped.

Tasha liked to sleep in the warm sun. She let me curl up right beside her as long as I didn't move too much. I liked that, so I behaved—well, most of the time.

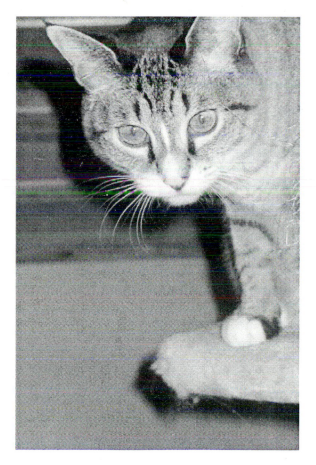

Tasha

At night, all crowded in Marilyn's bed, Tasha let me sleep with her but insisted that Marilyn and I sandwich her between us. If not, those sky blue eyes glowed red in the reflected moonlight. Several long meows followed until she had her way.

Another cat, Harrison, was more into the chasing game. Harrison was a black cat that looked as if someone had dipped him in a bucket of white paint, for his bottom half was pure as the Arctic snow, except for one black spot on the inside of each leg and a round black spot in the middle of his tummy. He had a white ring around his neck, with several white hairs randomly scattered on his otherwise black coat. He sported a little black beard on his completely white mouth, and had one white-tipped ear. His eyes were so crossed that it made me laugh every time I looked at him.

Harry

"Burmese" and "snowshoe" were terms I heard Marilyn use to describe him. Burmese or not, he was fun to chase until, of course, Marilyn caught me. She didn't always catch me. Lots of exercise both for the cat and me resulted. That cat could run faster than you could say "mom" backwards.

So now you have met my new Vashon Island family. I had become part of it.

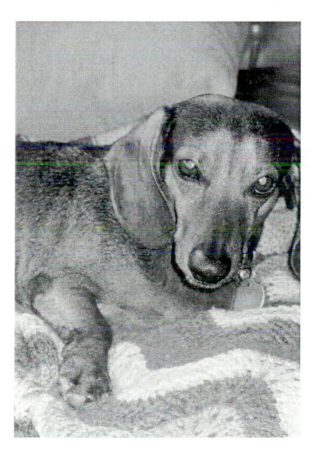

Schultzie

Chapter 2

Harrison, A Baddy Burmese!

We moved that summer. Marilyn's new log house would be built the following spring; in the meantime, she had to leave our beach house.

We spent part of the following year with Marilyn in a cabin on another beach but still on Vashon Island. The rest of the time we lived on a vacant lot a few miles away.

Harrison, Marilyn's half black-half white, cross-eyed big Burmese cat, sometimes known as Harry, used to sleep up in the neighbor's abandoned barn. It was a miniature barn, and had housed one horse long ago, but then I am getting ahead of my tale.

It all began when Marilyn bought a piece of property near where Vashon Island and Maury Island meet. The first thing to go up was a small greenhouse. In it she began storing shovels and rakes and other gardening things along with the cats' beds. The window stayed open when she was gone. Nearby, Marilyn had a large pen built for us dachsies.

And, you guessed it, the cats spent their evenings in the comfort of the greenhouse. When Marilyn was gone, we had wonderful care from another woman who loved animals, but we were always glad to see Marilyn when

Harrison

she came home from her work trips to Alaska.

Near the pen was an abandoned red barn. When he discovered the barn, Harrison climbed the outside steps. He hid out in the upper loft where a stash of straw made a nice warm bed. When Marilyn finally caught on to where he hid she would climb the ladder and catch him. And it was back to the beach cabin when she was home. The only time I accompanied her was memorable for both Harrison and Marilyn.

Somewhat late one day, Marilyn, having already picked up my uncles and dad, took me back over to the property. She located Tasha earlier but couldn't find Harrison.

Once there she pierced the air with her "kitty, kitty, kitty, here kitty" call—an immediate promise of some fun things to follow. Harrison wasn't about to come out with me there, but Marilyn didn't know that.

The neighbor man yelled down. "There's a black and white cat hiding up in the barn."

I stopped short and watched with growing interest as Marilyn ascended the steps to the loft area. Blood surged through my veins. Sure enough, she emerged with Harrison in her arms. She came down those steps gingerly, holding him in one arm and the ladder in the other. My hairs stood on end from what I smelled. My breathing came short and fast. My mouth went dry.

Patiently I waited at the bottom watching Harry's tail swish. Marilyn continued getting closer and closer. Finally, she jumped from the last rung to the ground.

That's when I made my move. With a deft upward leap I took a little bite at Harry's tail. Oh, it was soft and warm and furry!

Every hair on Harry's body bristled. He doubled his size. His phosphor-yellow eyes blazed. He yowled, and snarled and howled. Fully extending all 20 claws he revealed a matched set of razor-sharp knives. In the wink of an eye he shot through Marilyn's arms, with me right behind him. I had a few pieces of fur still stuck between my teeth. The chase was on.

We were out of sight before Marilyn said a word. Then I heard a scream and a yell of pain but kept right after that wonderful soft black tail.

I leaped, running as fast as my legs would go. I was almost up to Harry now. Then he made a supreme sprint, leaving me behind. The distance increased as we dashed through the woods. Then ….

Nothing! Nothing at all.

No tail. No Harry, just some deep scratchy brush.

Then silence. Even the birds stopped singing. I tried to get that cat's scent, but somewhere he had gone airborne, and that's when I lost it.

I heard Marilyn yell "Schultz!" Not seeing Harry's crossed eyes smoldering from the tree above, I rummaged around in the bushes, getting stickers in my hair. My nose itched from the stinging nettles. No aroma. No trace. No cat. I decided I had enough and returned to Marilyn. My left ear had a huge blackberry thorn stuck right into it. Blood gushed down my face as I shook my ears to rid myself of the thing.

Marilyn's arm was covered with blood as well. She seemed pale in contrast. She scooped me up, put me in the car, and we returned to the beach cabin in haste. Marilyn said little on the way.

She washed her arm and my ear with hydrogen peroxide and went to bed. I told my uncles what had happened. Moose's eyes glistened with envy as I described each moment Harry's tail waved in front of me as he was brought closer and closer down the ladder. All five of us climbed into bed with Marilyn. Dad just shook his head telling me I should have known better. After all, Marilyn liked her cats.

Marilyn seemed to get really hot during the night, sweating, and obviously was sick. The next morning her *cat fever* continued, but she left the cabin anyway, stuffing all of us in the car. Tasha ended up staying home alone. And, of course, Harrison was still on the beach property, probably enjoying the nice breakfast Marilyn left for him. We went uptown where Marilyn ordered lunch.

Eventually, Marilyn caught up with Harrison, but without any of us dachsies helping her.

To this very day Harrison stalks me, startling me as he leaps from behind a cabinet, or jumps out from half-closed doors then takes off. He has blood in his eyes when he sees me. I usually just yip, hoping Marilyn's nearby because I know if Harry ever caught me ... I don't want to think about it.

Chapter 3

New Family Members and Great Escapes

Life continued, with us camping in the pen when Marilyn was working in Alaska. When she came home, we went to the beach cabin with her. However, Marilyn never took me again when she went after the cats.

She put an old sleeping bag in one of our doghouses and kept food and water in the other one. The bedroom where we snoozed was nice and cozy. We slept, making a big dachsie pile. The door was small, so it kept the wind and rain out. Besides, Marilyn had rigged a second roof of metal keeping the whole area over both rooms from getting wet.

Marilyn learned early in the year from the vet that Baron had congestive heart failure, so she located a friend with a Great Dane named Blue Shadow Niki. This friend dachshund-sat Baron while Marilyn was in Alaska. By all accounts Niki lay down with Baron between her huge front paws. The two got their heads together. That way they were eyeball to eyeball in order to talk to each other. Baron needed medication twice a day, so Niki's mistress introduced the idea of treats to go along with those awful-tasting meds. Niki to this day insists on her treats since she had to have something along with Baron.

At other times Marilyn took Baron over to the dog sitter's house where he slept in the woman's bed at night and played during the day with a great bouncy, happy-go-lucky black lab named Boomer. Then one morning Baron climbed out of bed and just died. Marilyn buried him under the huge Maple tree on her property.

It was the end of February, and we were quite into a routine, until Marilyn brought home two unruly girls she rescued from a village in the Aleutians. It was then that we dubbed our pen the "puppy pen."

The girls were griffon pointer mixes, mother a purebred and dad a Heinz 57 of unknown parentage.

Oh, they were cute puppies when they first arrived; woolly, warm and cuddly. I guess Marilyn had a thing about black and white, because now, in addition to Harrison, we had these two puppies, also black and white on the bottom, except there were sort of black spots on their legs and belly, more like hunting spaniels. They started growing and soon were larger than either me or my uncles or even my dad.

Officially named Tosca and Lucia, after two well-known opera soprano roles, we called them "little piggies" because of their roundness as well as their insatiable appetites. Once their dinners were finished, they came after ours, so we began eating faster and faster. A dachshund could get indigestion that way.

Marilyn had some nice little trees planted in that puppy pen. Tosca and Lucia ate them.

Then one afternoon, I realized that, awkward or not, they could climb over the fence. At first it was with a great deal of effort, but it gradually became easier. I watched with mounting interest because I knew I could do the same thing.

Tosca, the friendlier of the two, showed me how to

go up and over the fence. I found it extremely difficult,

Tosca and Lucia

and the wires cut into my toes. With persistence, however, I finally managed it, as did Duff.

Both of us were worn out. Much too much effort! So I decided to show the girls how to dig under the fence. They had the brawn, but then I had the brains. Getting either of them to dig was easy, and their feet were perfect for the job.

We'd hide a bone at a strategic location. With those backhoes for paws, the girls dug enough so that in no time at all the four of us had a tunnel allowing all of us to escape. We lost several bones that way, until we hit upon an ingenious plan of calling their attention to a cat walking by.

Occasionally, one of Marilyn's cats would go by and disappear into the brush, but that didn't happen often enough for our purposes. So I'd bark with excitement, and sure enough the girls became alert, and would immediately go to the fence and after the cat. Most of the time, of course, there was no cat, but they didn't know it.

Maybe they caught a scent of one, or the breeze rustled a leaf or two. The bone would be forgotten, and off they would run after the phantom cat. One of us would collect the bone for future use, hide it for safe keeping with dad, then casually walk under the fence where moments before the girls had dug. Dad made it convenient by going into his doghouse to nap. He didn't care for all the activity, and definitely enjoyed the peace and quiet of those days when we were out hiding bones and chasing ghost cats.

The dog sitter came by and incarcerated us regularly, but in no time at all we were out again. Barriers were placed both above and below the fence making it more difficult. Sometimes it was raining, so we didn't leave the pen. But other times, when the sun was shining, out we would go, always finding a way through the maze of our prison.

Oftentimes the neighbor man caught us. Then he would bring over a few more boards and shore up our efforts. The fence became thicker at the bottom and higher and harder to escape from with each passing week. In addition to the boards, gravel and rocks were added to the bottom of the fence, and wire at the top.

Marilyn's rescued dogs became known as her two delinquent girls. Her nephew called them the "Hounds from Hell." We were more than glad to let them take all the blame for our escapes.

Tosca—All Innocence

Lucia relaxing under the Maple tree

Chapter 4

Guard Dogs! I Don't Think So!

One day Marilyn arrived home for the summer. Next thing we knew we were moving out of the cabin into a *tent, a real tent!*

The canvas was placed on a platform the contractors built right under the huge Maple tree on the other side of the puppy pen. Next to it stood a cylindrical thing that was supposed to be a shower. It never really worked.

The girls were collared and tied to a long dog run, much to their disappointment, and we were left to our own devices.

Excitement began when trucks and construction workers started coming almost daily. Marilyn had all she could do to keep us from getting in the way.

At first some of the workers were a little apprehensive. After all, having 16 feet, all belonging to dachshund bodies, was scary. Dad spent his days in the tent snoozing. Moose enjoyed sleeping as well, but came out to be with Duff and me. The three of us played and were constantly into mischief. In particular, we enjoyed sneaking up to the girls, taking a quick nip at their tails, and then dashing just out of reach. Their long line ran from the Maple tree to the neighbor's red barn.

None of us ever allowed Marilyn to sleep in, as we had to announce each worker's arrival just to keep them honest. Didn't want any slackers on the crew! When the delivery trucks full of lumber and logs arrived, we had to make sure Marilyn knew about them as well. At night, I checked out what had been done during the day. Every job, after all, needs a night foreman.

That summer Marilyn took pictures, watched, dreamed, and spent hours over the grill in front of her tent roasting corn, hamburgers, potatoes, and whatever else that sounded good to her. She even decorated the path right up to her "front door." Oh, yes, she had a kind of cooler in front, and a plug-in refrigerator along the side. Sometimes the refrigerator worked and sometimes it didn't. Inside the tent she had a television set, several bookshelves with some books, her phone and a cot.

The second night, we vaulted onto the cot, along with Marilyn, and when she picked up my dad, it collapsed in an agglomeration of dachsie tails, Marilyn and bedding. Barks, growls and a few groans hit the night air with resounding authority. She never fixed the cot, muttering the whole time something about dogs.

With the cot flattened and full of blankets and a sleeping bag handy, we didn't have to jump. I found this a lot more convenient, and so did dad. He didn't even have to pretend anymore. When he wanted to go to bed, he just burrowed down to the bottom of Marilyn's sleeping bag.

Some of her wool blankets ended up looking like Swiss cheese. That was because Duff liked to eat wool. Personally, I prefer cat tails—black ones at that, if you know what I mean.

The workers took a liking to the girls and came over to feed them part of their sandwiches at lunch. If we timed it just right, there were always bites for us as well. Marilyn discouraged this, particularly when it came to dad. By the time the summer was over, I think those workmen brought extra sandwiches for all of us to enjoy.

20

The girls were almost full-grown by mid-summer, or at least I thought they were. In reality, they were no more than jealous adolescents hitting their growth spurt. Stronger by the minute, they decided we dachshunds had the best of both worlds—being dogs and living like humans. That spelled trouble. I knew there was no telling what they would do next, so all of us kept outside their reach. It was particularly fun, though, to bait them, and run yipping to get Marilyn's attention in case the line holding them broke. That was when Marilyn bought a reinforced covered wire for their run.

One night, sound asleep in the tent, we heard a terrible crash nearby. Marilyn thought it was the girls, and shot outside to find them emerging from their doghouses barking crazily.

She looked around and saw that the temporary outhouse had *fallen down.*

It didn't fall down by itself. There wasn't a breath of air stirring. The girls couldn't reach the outhouse from their run. Marilyn was on the phone in moments calling the emergency number 911. Both girls continued their bedlam of noise.

Down below through the trees I spotted a couple of figures running and laughing. The bushes hid them from Marilyn's view, but not from my nose or ears. I snickered because I knew their route took them right through a large patch of stinging nettles and thorny, nasty blackberry bushes. They wouldn't be smiling when those vines grabbed them as they made their escape.

Duff and I wanted to give chase. Marilyn kept a firm hold on both of us. The girls continued to bark, howl, wail, lament and make every kind of noise they could. Their bellowing didn't stop.

The police arrived. What excitement! High adventure! Flashing lights! Policemen searching the partially completed building. I guess they thought there might be someone lingering there.

And through it all the two girls persevered with their wailing.

The female police officer tried to get Marilyn to quiet them. No victory for Marilyn. More of embarrassment, I should think, than anything else. After all, the girls were on guard duty and failed to warn us of approaching problems. It was Tosca and Lucia who should have been embarrassed.

It was 12:30 in the morning when the police pulled away. Marilyn fed each of the girls some delicious morsel just to keep them quiet. By this time I am sure it didn't make much difference, as I think every neighbor within a five mile radius was awake.

Later, much later, someone told Marilyn there were hundreds of outhouses, all from the same company, that had been turned over in the greater Seattle area.

And that's the way our summer went.

Lucia

Tosca

Chapter 5

The Secret of Toilet Training

Occasionally, I'll backslide when it comes to potty training, but only when I really want to punish Marilyn, and that's infrequent. When she leaves me for one of her work trips to Alaska, however, I leave my message as to what I think about it, much to her daughter's annoyance.

You see, my dad and my uncles took me under their tutelage from that first day on the island and showed me the ropes as to where to go to the bathroom, and it wasn't in the house. Then one by one they left for the Rainbow Bridge, that place where all dachsies go when they die.

I'm the only dachshund Marilyn has left. We share the log house, now completed, with the cats, and, of course, there are the two girls, who live outside.

Marilyn's daughter has moved in with us while she is finishing her physical therapy internship. I really annoy her because I bark at her every time she comes home. Oh, well, we can't please everyone.

Chapter 6

Fur Balls and Fluff

A year after the house was finished, Marilyn came home one afternoon with another cat. I heard comments to her son Jhon about it being a Himalayan.

Jhon just groaned. "Too many animals, you have just too many." Jhon, however, plays more with this cat than any of the others on his visits.

All I know is that this fur ball had more fluff than any two cats I had ever seen. Marilyn named her "Chandalar" after a small but beautiful river in Alaska. No more opera singers, although this one could definitely qualify, as she was not hesitant in letting everyone know what she wanted with her high-pitched meows. She was particularly persistent when Marilyn brought her in at night and wouldn't let her back out.

The local pet protector's group had rescued her after she had been on the run for several months. No one claimed her as their cat. VIPP (Vashon Island Pet Protectors) had the local vet check her out, then put her up for adoption. She had worms, not just regular tape worms, but round worms requiring more medication.

Chandalar

Well, Chandalar wasn't like most cats, and particularly not at all like Harrison. I couldn't intimidate this new one at all. In fact, she walked right up to me, and started smelling me just as any dog would do. It was then that I decided she just might be a dog masquerading as a cat. With all that fur she could be hiding anything.

When Marilyn called us, indicating dinner was served, Chandalar raced me to the food dish. The two of us would almost trip Marilyn on our way, leaving a trail of fur balls and matted hair everywhere.

Chandalar howled every evening for Marilyn to let her back out once she had eaten. When the lights were turned off, she quieted.

Sometimes, when Jhon was over, he would forget and leave a door open. Out Chandalar charged.

During the spring months she brought in enough seed pods to start a garden—all caught in her fur.

But that's not all she brought back.

Chandalar was an incredible hunter. She stalked the neighbor's field every day and night when she escaped. She was the terror, the monster to all kinds of critters. When the grass was mowed, she'd sit in the middle of the field just waiting for some poor creature to twitch a whisker alerting her to its presence. The stalk was over, and the chase begun. Although it wasn't a chase really, as Chandalar almost always won. There were rats, and mice, moles and voles. There were big ones and little ones and ones all sizes between. She found them all.

She brought her catches into the house, deposited them under the dining room table on Marilyn's good Turkish rug, then went out to hunt some more. Usually she ate just part of her catch, much to Marilyn's dismay.

Now I liked to hunt but didn't have her patience. I guess she knew this. We had a mutual admiration for one another. On occasion, she brought in an extra furry critter for me, hunt me down, and give it to me uneaten. I guess she figured Marilyn didn't feed me enough.

One morning Chandalar hadn't been out more than ten minutes when she came back in with about a six-inch long body of warm fur and a little short tail. She hadn't eaten any of it, but called me, then presented me with the critter. It was quite dead, but there were no marks on it anywhere. I think Chandalar must have scared to death whatever it was.

Marilyn groaned, picked it up and deposited it on the other side of the fence in a hole where I couldn't get it. She wasn't sure what particular critter the thing had been. It wasn't a mouse and definitely not a rat, as the tail was far too short and the head shaped differently. A trip to the library revealed that the creature was a meadow vole.

Having been introduced to this type of critter, I smelled one under the couch in the sunroom the next morning. It must have crawled in through an open door. Or, more likely, Chandalar thought I should have some fun and brought it in *on the hoof* so to speak. My nose commanded me to follow it all around the couch. My quivering body alerted Marilyn that something was under there, so she moved the furniture. A furry body scooted out.

A quick jump, I had it, and immediately dispatched it into history.

"Schultz!" That tone of voice meant Marilyn did not think too highly of my actions.

She picked up this latest furry critter, and realized it was the same thing as the one Chandalar had brought me the previous day. It went outside as well to an unknown place where I couldn't get to it.

On occasion, Chandalar just left a catch for me to find, while she hurried off to resume her hunting. I always investigated but sometimes didn't find the remains for days, like the rat in the far end of the driveway.

Quiet unexpectedly, I sniffed it out, pushed it with my nose, then rolled on top of it. I tried to make sure my neck and shoulders had direct contact with the carcass. The aroma was overwhelming. I wanted to mask my dachshund odor; then I would have an advantage in the chase of some future critter. Chandalar might even be fooled, but I doubted it.

"Schultz!"

Oh, oh! Marilyn spotted me before I finished my final toss of the rat. My left shoulder still needed anointing. No time. Caught in the act.

Marilyn carted me into the house holding me at a discrete distance. Not good.

The quick trip upstairs was even more ominous. I squirmed all the way, to no avail.

The bathroom door was shut. No escape. Trapped.

Already Marilyn had water running.

All too quickly the tub was filled with warm water, just to a dachshund level, in order to get me good and wet.

Now what's this?

Off came my collar, and in I went. All of me.
Marilyn soaped me up good with dog shampoo. Then
scrubbed me down with more soap after a quick rinse
with water spraying in every direction. Out I emerged
after a second showering with cold water. She dried me
off with a gigantic towel. That towel was soft and clean.
But by then, so was I. No more rat perfume. Next came
my collar.

How come Chandalar didn't get this treatment?

I knew the answer before I asked. Chandalar always
centered her attention on something fresh, not ones

partially rotten. And that was the difference. Chandalar wasn't really a dachshund disguised as a cat after all. She didn't like old dead things at all. I loved them.

Chapter 7

Travels with Marilyn

Marilyn put my black leash into the front seat of the car along with my favorite blanket. Next came dog food and a big bottle of water. Now that meant more than an up-town-to-get-the-groceries trip. Hmmmmmm!

Her bag casually tossed in the back seat, was followed by "Here, Schultzie, c'mon, come. Let's go!"

That's all I needed to hear. My ears flopped as I skidded down the seven steps, and dove into the car, right up to the front seat. I chased my tail a couple of times then curled up in my blanket. We were off. I let the sun and the car's even hum lull me to sleep until we arrived at the ferry landing.

Then up to the window, I startled the deck hand with a fierce bark just as he was directing Marilyn to park the car on the ferry. Another bark escaped before he moved to the next car. He laughed and kept going.

My head went out the window. The wind off Puget Sound lifted my ears just a little as the ferry left the dock. Salty air greeted my nostrils. The breeze felt cold against my nose. I looked down at the oil-splashed deck, then my eyes caught a gull as it flew alongside the boat, keeping pace for at least five minutes. I pulled back inside, circled three times and made a little nest in my blanket and closed my eyes.

The captain blew the whistle for landing—one long and two short blasts. I hear the announcement, "Now arriving Point Defiance," and pushed my nose through the window just in time to see the crewman direct our car off the vessel. Marilyn continued up the hill. That's when I buried my head in my blanket for a long nap.

I awoke much later with a start. My belly told me lunchtime was long past. I didn't eat any of my dog food. Hopefully, if I held out long enough, Marilyn would stop and serve something more interesting. The highway seemed endless.

Occasionally, we stopped. Marilyn, leaving the car for one reason or another, signaled me to make my move. My food dish was dumped. The contents quickly buried under the front car seat with my nose.

Out of sight, out of mind! Marilyn didn't catch on at first.

Longer stops meant restaurants. That's when I would gaze into her eyes. Downcast. Starved hound dog. I was so hungry. After all, she was leaving me in the car and going in to have something to eat.

Those leftover bits of hamburgers, omelets, baked potatoes—whatever Marilyn had ordered in the restaurants—were treasured meals. I particularly enjoyed it when she ordered cheddar cheese topping on the potatoes, and, of course, with a little meat on the side.

Most of the time I slept while she drove. Stopping for gas was not particularly interesting except when we drove through Oregon. There it is a state law that attendants had to fill the tank rather than the self-serve stations we visited in other nearby states.

My guard-dog instincts emerged at these stations, particularly when she left the car to go in and pay. Most of the attendants ignored me, but not all of them.

Marilyn's return usually found me in a dizzy dachsie discourse with a red-faced station hand looking properly admonished.

Then there was the police officer, also in Oregon, who stopped us. He looked especially fearsome, and Marilyn was most upset. So I told him in no uncertain barks what I thought. I think that is something Marilyn would just as soon forget.

When Marilyn left the car for meals, paying gas attendants or some other necessity, I discovered a little entertainment. After all, this hound dog didn't want to become bored. It so happens that her car had a little red button between the front two seats. Walking across to the driver's seat when Marilyn left the car with me in it, I found that stepping right in the middle of the button produced flashing green lights on the dashboard. Watching those lights at first was fun, but then I would get tired and curl up in her seat.

Occasionally those green flashing lights would be a sure way to get Marilyn to come back to the car immediately. She'd hit the red button, mumble something at me, then disappear.

One evening Marilyn and her nephew Scott went to eat at a Thai restaurant in Bend, Oregon, and left me in the car. The nerve of them.

I managed to *accidentally* step on the red button between the seats. It produced the predicted response: flashing green lights.

That evening I had Marilyn come out to the car five times before she put my emptied dog-food bowl upside down over that button. When she and Scott finally emerged, she had a little carry-out box of wonderful morsels. I could get used to Thai food. It was a little on the hot side, but not bad, especially the chicken.

Another more memorable occasion also happened in Oregon, and that time Marilyn didn't catch on to me until it was too late.

We met Marilyn's good friend Marian in Ashland,

Oregon, for the Shakespeare Festival. The two of them stayed in a nice Bed and Breakfast that didn't allow animals. Can you imagine, not allowing me to go inside?

Marilyn took me out for a nice long, evening walk, said good night, gave me a big hug, and left me in the car with the windows open for lots of fresh night air (more than I really wanted), a bowl full of water and another one full of food, dog food. Yuk!

I turned around in my blanket several times, settled down, then decided I wasn't quite ready for sleep. With a big stretch I crossed over to Marilyn's seat, and carelessly put one of my front feet down hard on the red button.

Green lights flashed.

It was really dark outside, and that made them all the brighter. The flashing was just like our Christmas tree, but it wasn't even October. Then I stood on the red button, and the lights stopped. Hmmmmm! Now this was kind of fun, and besides there was this wonderful clicking noise. I didn't feel quite so alone. Returning to the passenger side of the car, I hit the button again. They stopped.

I walked back over to Marilyn's seat and stepped on the red button again. Sure enough, the green lights flashed and clicked just like the old clock we had at home. They looked kind of neat in the middle of the night. Everything else was jet-black outside like the inside of a black cat. But in the car I stepped on the button again, and everything inside the car became dark inkiness.

Next, I carefully went back over to my side, and put one foot on the button. After all, the iridescence of the green lights was better than black darkness.

I scratched the seat, turned around three more times and burrowed into my blanket for the night. The soft click click click of the lights as they flashed off and on was soothing. I closed my eyes, hearing their muted click. I curled into a tighter ball after nosing my way even further into my blanket and fell fast asleep. The distant sound of clicking became one with the flying bugs coming in through the windows. Buried as I was the insects would never find me.

The stillness was shattered by Marilyn's voice, "Oh, no!"

I woke up with a start to find it was day. Night had disappeared.

Now, what was she complaining about? After all, I had spent the night in the car, while she had a nice, warm, comfortable bed. I had slept with the cool night air and all matter of biting pests chasing me right under my blanket while she slept behind screened windows. I had nothing but dog food for a midnight snack, while she had gourmet rolls and juice and no telling what other delicacies.

I watched with growing interest as Marian came up behind her. The two of them began talking. Marilyn got in the car, turned the key. Nothing. The engine didn't roar, it didn't even turn over. Of course, the green lights had long ago faded and stopped blinking their on and off, on and off, on and off.

Marilyn seemed disturbed. She said something most unkind about me. Marian snickered. Marilyn put my leash on. We walked for my morning outing, but not before she made a telephone call. This time I thought best to humor her, so I did my business. The tour around the garden was much briefer than last night's walk. She stuffed me hurriedly back in the car, and left.

Some time passed before a big white truck pulled up next to our car. A great, burley man got out. I barked. He laughed as he pulled out some heavy-duty wires and went under the hood of our vehicle.

Marilyn came out. "Schultz!"

The man asked her what happened.

"Oh, Schultzie likes to step on the switch for the emergency lights. He usually turns them off before he's through, but this time he left them on."

"That's the first time I've heard that story" the Triple A emergency service (American Automobile Association) man commented, smiling as he charged the battery then started the car.

Oh, as I yawned then curled up to go back to sleep, I thought this was "much ado about nothing."

Chapter 8

More Travels with Marilyn

Marian was always fun to visit in San Francisco. While she didn't have any dogs, she had several cats, all of which were strictly indoor felines.

Several times I was able to visit at Marian's house, with Marilyn, of course, accompanying me. Marian would lock her cats in her bedroom during the day, and Marilyn and I would stay in the guest bedroom at night, so I never got a chance to see the cats, except an occasional paw or two under the door. Even without the paws, my nose told me there were three of them.

The most recent trip occurred when Marilyn drove down this past December for a few days. We arrived in nasty weather. Misty. Cold. Wet. Foggy. Awful.

Despite the weather, Marilyn dragged me from that nice comfortable Victorian house onto the wet pavement and pouring rain every morning. She expected me to take care of my business. Worse, she would follow me around with a little plastic bag. Of course, I'd pee on just about every tree. Who wouldn't with all those dog smells. Fire hydrants weren't in convenient locations. I marked my passage with care. But spending the time standing on all that cement with water running off the nearby buildings right where I stood, and Marilyn hovering over me ready with a scupper was not my idea of doing business. I'd wait thank you very much.

Sooner or later Marilyn would give up.

It was back to Marian's house. Oh yes, I forgot to say Marian had beautiful wool Oriental carpets all over her house. Several of them were in the living room. Best of all that room was closest to the door, and furthermost from the kitchen.

These rugs were soft and warm, and made just for a little dog like me. My favorite was a medium-sized bluish-brown one in front of Marian's piano. My nose told me the cats enjoyed this particular runner as well. It was out of the main flow of traffic, slightly out of the line of sight as people walked by into the rest of the house, and even softer than the rest. The colors shaded any little objects that happened to get left there. And that was important.

Marilyn always headed into the kitchen once we returned from one of those morning walks. I'd shiver and shake, ridding myself of the extra moisture and shaking just a little longer than I really needed. Marilyn went for the kitchen.

I'd linger in the living room, just for a couple of moments, and just long enough to empty my bowels right in the middle of that little soft wool runner. Then, like a flash, I would go to the kitchen to see if I could catch a cat or get a morsel to eat. Marian's room was close to the kitchen, and I could play with those cats' paws under the door. Of course, Marilyn would be distracted, and not discover my calling card in the living room until much later. When she did, she never knew exactly when I had left it. The first time she accidentally stepped in it.

During the next three mornings she was more careful to discover those little brown sausage-like piles before she walked across the rug.

One evening while we were there, several friends dropped by to visit and have dinner. Marian wanted me to stay in the bedroom rather than be around the table.

Well, okay!

So I whimpered and carried on, but to no avail. Marian really didn't want me in the eating area, so I stayed in the bedroom. And, of course, I continued to let them know how abused I was throughout the meal.

Marian's upstairs neighbor heard the whole commotion and was sucked right in to my ploy for sympathy. He bitterly complained about Marilyn leaving me alone, didn't want to hear my tortured feelings of abandonment, and stated clearly that he felt she was abusive.

Marilyn was happy to leave San Francisco on that occasion. And I was forced to do my duty back on the streets and in the rest stops between there and Vashon Island. How humiliating!

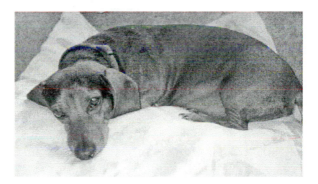

Chapter 9

Rescuing Golf Balls

Marilyn's daughter Natalia stayed in Welches, near Mount Hood, for the summer with some friends while she worked between school semesters. We visited her a couple of times.

The afternoon we drove down, people conversed and didn't pay much attention to me. Natalia was at work part of the time.

The house was large and, best of all, had a huge yard filled with interesting hiding places. A big golden lab named Holly lived there, and usually there were one or two other visiting dogs.

Holly was different. She showed me around the place. Since she was much older, she soon grew tired of my enthusiasm, wagged her tail and lay down on the deck to nap in the warm sun. Then a couple of the other dogs appeared, ruining my fun. Worse, they were bigger than I am.

During Holly's tour I discovered two things, however, that turned the tables. First of all, I could get under the porch and the other dogs couldn't. Secondly, there were these little white balls in the garage, just the right size for me to carry. There was a whole bucket of them.

When one of the other dogs came near, I shot right under the porch with my newly found ball. They growled and snarled but couldn't reach me, nor could they reach the ball. I lay down with it, just a nose away, looking at those envious dogs. Soon they realized I wasn't coming out.

Time passed. The bigger dogs left and started playing in the yard. That's when I sneaked out. Then they spotted me again; I had a ball they wanted. The chase began. I dashed right back under the porch clutching my prize firmly in my teeth.

Soon they tired of waiting. Holly woke up and began playing as well. I came out to join the fun, when the big dogs spotted me again. I never let the porch get far away, and was soon back under it with the little white ball clutched tightly out of reach from those dogs. They didn't waste too many barks this time. I patiently waited. Sure enough, they were back sniffing around, playing in the high grass and enjoying the hot summer sun.

Out I came. Then the chase began again. I lost no time in getting back to my secure refuge. This began to be fun. They barked and barked. I yawned, always keeping my nose just a paw's distance from the ball, and, of course, well out of their reach.

I was sorry when those other dogs went home. Shortly after they left, Marilyn emerged from the house. "Schultz," she called opening the car door for me. Reluctantly, I got in. Marilyn said her good-byes and we left.

Not long after, we were back in Welches, but only briefly. The subject of golf came up. The people owning the house found a whole cache of golf balls under their porch, and apparently had a terrible time getting them out because no one could fit under the deck.

I overheard the people tell Marilyn that Natalia lay
down on the grass, and with a long pole was finally able
to reach under and pull out the golf balls one at a time.
I'll bet she was not a happy camper as she fished for
each one. I am sure her words were not fit for this little
hound dog's ears.

I went outside. Sure enough, I checked and there
wasn't one of my prized balls left where I had deposited
them. Now, you know who has the attitude.

Chapter 10

A Dachshund Stand Off

Waldport. That's a small town somewhere along Oregon's coast. Marilyn and I were visiting. The time was late one evening. Everyone was sitting in comfortable chairs around a nice roaring fire, everyone that is, except me. Ed, Leslie and Marilyn were exchanging stories, snacking, and enjoying a glass of wine.

I can tell you right now that I wasn't one of Ed's favorites from the first moment he laid eyes on me, but he didn't say anything. In fact, I don't think he likes little dogs at all, particularly ones that chased the resident cat. He just didn't appreciate the fact that I wasn't really a dog, but rather a dachshund, and there is a difference.

Ed was sitting in the biggest and most comfortable chair in the house, and I was sitting—on the floor! The chair was his, and no one sat in it except Ed. Everyone there knew that.

Then Ed left for the kitchen, and that's when I made my move.

The chair just invited me to sit in it. I nimbly jumped up into it, turned around several times and settled down for a nice comfortable nap. This was more like it.

The hum in Marilyn and Leslie's voices stopped when Ed returned. One eye opened. I yawned. Then opened both eyes. I gave him one of my "not on your life am I going to move" looks. He gave me an "oh, yes you are" look right back, and stood his ground.

I turned around in the chair again and made myself even more comfortable keeping one eye on Ed.

He stood there quietly for several minutes just looking at me. Nose to nose I glared back at him and wiggled my butt down into the chair even more. The moments hung in the air. The crackling of the fire was the only sound in the room. Light patterns danced on the ceiling. I didn't get up. Ed continued to stand. I twitched a shoulder.

And then he did it.

He barked.

He sounded just like a big dog. This great big over-6-feet-2-inches-tall man barked his funny challenge, and at me, a tiny little beast only weighing 15 pounds.

Annoyed at Ed, and even more so at Leslie and Marilyn for laughing so hard, I sighed and got out of the chair.

I walked right out of the room looking for the cat. The next morning when I found that cat I chased her up a tree in Leslie's yard just to show who was boss. Leslie had an awful time getting her down.

Chapter 11

Pee, Poop and Prairie Dogs

This time we were returning from Wyoming. It was another one of Marilyn's car adventures, and all because of some friend's wedding in Jackson Hole! That meant we drove through Washington, then traversed Idaho's panhandle, part of Montana, more of Idaho and then through the Snake River Gorge into Wyoming.

Before the wedding Marilyn let me run all around the neighboring field. No rain, but no mice either. It was when I spotted a jogger that Marilyn put back my leash and we returned to the car.

Since I wasn't the main attraction that day, Marilyn had removed my leash, opened the windows and left me inside while she went into the church. At least I got to greet the bride after the ceremony. She was dressed all in white and gave me a big hug. Oh, that felt good. I would have liked to stay around for a few more hugs, but Marilyn dragged me back to the car.

Then it was return through Idaho, this time through the southern part crossing into Oregon's sagebrush and rattlesnake country. And, finally, back to Washington.

Now that's a lot of travel for a dachshund in four days. I slept most of the time, but not all of it.

Idaho particularly seemed forever. Then we parked at one of those rest stops that make little dogs go to the pet area on a leash. Out came my black leash before the engine was even turned off.

A good time to fribble the minutes away. I didn't lift my leg. Nor did I straighten my tail and hunch my back followed by a giant push of my insides. No peeing or pooping. I had other agendas.

There was a picnic table nearby, and some interesting smells coming from the short grass and dirt directly ahead of me. Peculiar little mounds dotted the grassy area.

Yiiiiiiiip. Yip. A yelp, humongous and unexpected. I sprung to full alert and peered around Marilyn's leg. There it was again. My neck swiveled toward the noise, in time to see a stout, short-tailed, short-legged what? A jump-yip display. Then it was gone.

Another high-pitched warning, barking cry, unlike any I had ever heard. And this time it was behind me. A quick pivot, and ... nothing. It was as though the second discord told the first hullabaloo that I was there. Each sound seemed slightly different and involved a variety of tones.

The ground under me seemed alive.

Then I noted a hole banked with earth. The piles of soil that formed strangle little conical shapes looked like miniature volcanoes. Only somebody built them.

I walked to the closest one and cautiously peered down. Dense darkness greeted me.

The odor emitted from that hole caught me full in the snout. Those little critters, whatever they were, had one big scent. Yuk! It was foul, fearsome and ferocious. Quickly I backed away, afraid the monster would emerge breathing fire.

Deep within I heard chirping alert calls, and scolding.

46

Off to the right, out of the corner of my eye, a buff-colored squirrel—or was it a rodent—appeared.

"Prairie dog." Marilyn uttered.

Then with a magician's quickness, prairie dog was gone.

Prairie dog. Hmmmmmmm!

Not a rodent at all, Marilyn later explained, and certainly not a dog; prairie dogs belong to the squirrel family. From the size of their heads, I decided these little guys down there somewhere in those tunnels were small ones, not fully grown. Juveniles. After all, we were there in early June. That's when the kids emerge from their coteries, or family groups, located deep within burrows their parents dig.

Quick as a wink, I shot toward the nearest hole.

Quicker than a blink, Marilyn pulled me back on my leash.

Choked, I gasped coming to an immediate and sudden halt inches away from the crater.

"Schultz, come."

The cavity beckoned.

No, not now. What a bummer.

Determined, Marilyn headed straight for the car without so much as a backward glance. I found myself airborne as she tugged my leash dragging me behind.

Once in the car she started the engine, and we shot back onto the main highway leaving a blast of dust and rocks behind us. It was then I had the urge to lift my leg.

Chapter 12

A Rescued Dachshund If Ever
There Was One

Benz Wolfgang Thomas is one of my pen pals from Alabama. His human mom, Zak (Mary Anne), even set him up with his own e-mail address so all of his buddies could write to him. Reading his messages I realized not all rescued dachshunds meant they went to new homes. Benz brought new meaning to the concept of "rescued."

His antics will bring a hoot and a holler to those who have a dachshund or two. Long-haired Benz is only eleven pounds, and his food intake is watched like a hawk. But even hawks sleep.

He learned early on how to jump on the garbage can foot pedal, which opened the lid so the contents were readily accessible. The garbage can was replaced. Chairs, tables, bookcases don't stop him. Between you and me, I think he is a disguised German mountain goat. But then I will let him tell you his story.

Both of my human brothers, Christopher and Charlie, came home last Sunday from the University of Alabama where they attend school. Since my human

Benz Wolfgang Thomas

mom did not want to cook, they decided to order Chinese take out from their favorite restaurant—New China. Hmmmmmmmmmm!

When it arrived, the smells—oh, so good!

All of them pigged out and enjoyed the Chinese, while MacGyver, the golden retriever, and I had the same old same old dried dog food.

Each whiff made my eyes roll with anticipation. I listened to the stories and drooled with each passing moment, hoping someone would slip a morsel to me. At long last they finished! Before any of them could clear all of the dishes I jumped on one of the chairs then on to the table. After all, they needed help trying to clean the plates. Besides, this way, the dishwasher would not have to do them.

Well, I got caught and did I get in trouble! Mom was not at all pleased with me!

Then I got back on the table after the food and dishes were gone. Little did my mom realize how sloppy my human brothers ate. Those spilled samples were delicious. Just the way I like Chinese.

I know I would have gotten some during the meal, but mom was watching my two human brothers very carefully. That was not good for me. She complained to them because the last few times they had been home I really chowed down on some good food, but then had to go to the vet because I scooted my butt across the floor, a sure indication that I needed my anal glands cleaned.

Hopefully, Schultz, you do not have to go through that embarrassing procedure to get the anal gland sacs emptied. The only good thing about it is that I get to see Dr. Heather McIntyre, my vet. She is a real sweetie as she has a mini smooth dachshund at home just like you. So I always get a good hug and kiss from her! Also, she is young, just out of vet school and cute! Christopher likes her too, but he is about three or four years younger than she is. I know that Christopher is jealous that I get all the hugs and kisses from Dr. McIntyre.

I particularly like chicken fried rice. One of Christopher's visits included a lot of take-out Chinese. Someone called him on the phone just as he came in the door with the food. He got on the portable phone, took it to another room and talked and talked and talked and talked. That time, I was able to sneak up on the table, remove one of those little boxes, and take it down under the table where I quietly ate it. No one realized what I had done, thinking the take-out place hadn't included the fried rice.

Much later mom discovered the empty box under the table, and of course, knew. I guess that's why she watches Christopher and Charlie so much when they bring food home.

That time I didn't hear her comments because I was

comfortably taking a little nap in the next room.

Some occasions I don't make it to the vet. Mom takes things into her own hands. Once, she stashed some Easter candy five feet off the ground on top of a bookcase—which wasn't too far away from a chair, then a table, and from there I was home free—I made a flying leap to the book case and pulled the bag down. The first to go was the sleeve of M&Ms with the blue bunny on top, and, of course, the M&Ms as well. I left the one with the yellow bunny, and instead went straight for the small Reese cups and ate them, foil and all.

That's when I got caught. Mom immediately pulled the book <u>Emergency First Aid For You Dog</u> off the bookshelf. Out came the milk, peroxide and the syringe and down it went, with me squirming the whole time. Then mom poured water, lots of water down me, and that's when I threw up. After three doses of this awful stuff mom had all of the chocolate out of me. I hid for about the next hour, then was ready to eat again. The Easter candy was, of course, long gone by then.

There are those pleasant full tummy times as well, when nothing really happens.

Mom had a large, eight-ounce rib eye steak that had been grilled the previous weekend. She took it out and was going to eat some of it, then put the rest back in the refrigerator. Well, she forgot that she had moved a chair by the counter top when she was putting a new tablecloth on our old round oak table. That little oversight, however, did not escape me.

The phone rang. That's when I made my move. I was able to get on the chair, then the counter top. Oh, that steak tasted so good. I ate it all. It was grilled to perfection. I did such a thorough job of cleaning the plate, mom thought she had left the steak in the refrigerator. Then she realized she hadn't. MacGyver was outside so he was not a suspect.

That's when mom checked my belly, and, of course, I was ready to pop. She knew I was the rascal. Her mood *wasn't very nice because she wanted to eat it too.*

Well, I knew if I hid for about 20 minutes, mom would come looking for me and everything would be okay again. Sure enough. Twenty minutes later there she was, calling...."Benz. Benz, come here! Benz."

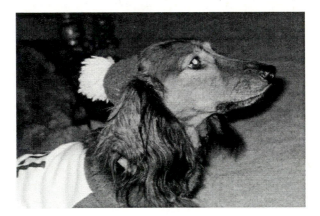

Benz in his Bama (University of Alabama) costume

Okay, it's mine, all mine!

Chapter 13

Starfish, Seahorses and Sand Dollars

My internet friend's propensity for food didn't stop with his human mother's cooking. Oh, no!

Benz took matters into his own paws when the basement flooded during a foundation repair job to the house. His golden retriever brother, MacGyver, joined him on this little gourmet adventure.

Shortly after the repair work began, the workmen hit the major water main. They didn't break it, just moved it enough to cause a nasty, steady little drip. Evaporation didn't keep up. Water on the floor. Panic!

His human mistress, Zak, frantically pulled boxes from the flowing waters in order to save some of her treasures: pine cones from years gone by, old specialty flower pots from her grandmother's house, and a large box of starfish and sand dollars and seahorses all from Florida's Gulf Coast where she had once gone scuba diving. These treasures had aged well, fifteen to twenty years at least. Oh, there were some shells too, in the bottom of the starfish box. But the aged fish jerky was the prize.

I'm not at all sure who rescued whom on this one. Maybe Benz can give us a clue.

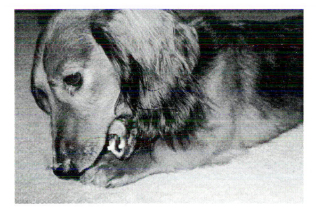

Benz

MacGyver

Gold mine! That's what it was. A real gold mine of gourmet delights—an entire box of dried fish. I salivated right on the spot. Stars danced before my eyes as I envisioned the delectable delights my nose told me were inside. And, best of all, my human mom was totally unaware of this little discovery.

I gave MacGyver a glowering look. Usually, he just sat on the porch waiting for me to get caught at whatever it was I wasn't supposed to be doing. This time he was clueless as to what we had stumbled upon, at least at first.

The six seahorses were gone in the wink of an eye. They crunched nicely as I ate them. The sand dollars just fell apart. They were small ones, maybe the size of a quarter, so I didn't care. But the starfish, now that was a different story. Some were the size of dinner plates, and some smaller but still a respectable size. I shared a couple of the little ones with MacGyver. What else could a little dog do to keep him quiet?

I grabbed onto a leg, and chewed to my heart's content. And when I had enough of that leg, there was always another one to begin gnawing on.

Well, there were way too many to finish off at one sitting.

That night Christopher, my human brother, commented about my salty, sweet breath. Unusual. A new toothpaste! Well, what do you expect from a fifteen-twenty year old starfish? But mom and Christopher had no idea of the snacks we were feasting on in the basement.

Mom opened up my mouth, checked my teeth, tongue, and even my throat. I almost choked my mouth was open so long. No clues remained. I smiled a dachshund smile, yawned, and went to bed. Since I didn't seem to be sick, mom didn't think much more about it until Christopher opened his big mouth again the next day about MacGyver's breath having the same salty, sweet smell. It was a mystery in both Christopher

56

and Mom's eyes. Now if MacGyver had just kept his cool, but he didn't.

During the day I hid in the garage with several starfish. It was cool in there and out of sight from all the repairmen's digging of ten-foot trenches around the house, and rain and clay filling up the holes as fast as they were dug. Mom was quite occupied. MacGyver, however, took his share of our bounty outside. He was missing some of his teeth so he had more difficulty chewing. He'd only nibble some, then save the rest for a snack later. The result was pieces of starfish strewn all over the lawn.

Mom spotted one of those body parts in the driveway, and watched as MacGyver lumbered right for it.

Then she knew. The mystery was solved. She gathered up what she found left, but, of course, most were missing body parts. And you know who got the blame for our little caper. I did. But then, after all, I have an excellent nose for things and that box was put down on the ground. I didn't even have to climb up for them.

Was she upset! I don't know if it was because she was worried that we ate them and we could get sick, or because we ate them and she had been saving them. I was in deep trouble.

Now you may think that was the end of the story, but just the other day mom found another starfish and only missing three legs. She put it into the den on top of her desk. Mistake!

That was an easy find.

I could have eaten the entire piece but it made too much noise as I chewed. I took it to the back of the house to my bedroom, but mom apparently heard the crunching sound or missed me and came looking. I got caught. Again!

She tried to get the pieces out of my mouth. MacGyver sauntered by, checked out the scene, nabbed *the remaining piece of starfish, and finished it off in one mouthful. The traitor!*

What neither mom nor MacGyver know is that I took a precaution by hiding two of the starfish legs in a place where no one will find them. This time I'm not sharing.

Chapter 14

Rescues Happen The World Over

Benz introduced me to some long-haired dachshunds in The Netherlands, and it was then I learned about Elroy. He's a silver dapped long hair, and now he belongs to Roelie and Tienco and lives with three other dachsies: his mom Moni, his aunt Nancy, and his twin sister Iris. On occasion, a wirehaired mini dachshund named Lotte comes to visit.

Ten years ago Elroy belonged to Roelie and Tienco as a pup and was sold to an older woman with the agreement that should something happen and she couldn't keep him, he would be welcomed back. Of course, no one ever expected he would be without a home at a future time.

At first Tienco and Roelie heard frequent news from Elroy's new family, and then nothing. Nine years passed, then one morning a telephone call came from the woman's son. He had to find a home for Elroy.

Roelie and Tienco explained they had agreed to take Elroy back years before, a promise the son knew nothing of. He revealed that his mother had Alzheimer's. Elroy's brother, the son's own dachsie, and Elroy

Elroy

fought, and Elroy would go after the grandchild. They couldn't have that. They couldn't keep Elroy. Clearly, the son was desperate to get rid of him. He didn't want to put Elroy in an animal shelter and was thankful and relieved Roelie and Tienco would take him back.

The son told Roelie that he and his wife went over daily to see his mother and check on Elroy. They found that Elroy piddled and pooped all over the house. He didn't have the right food, and sometimes he was out of food altogether. His water dish was often empty. His long hair was a mess of tangles. The hair on his ears was so snarled it was difficult to see where it began and his skin left off.

They knew the mother could not keep him. The woman who loved Elroy so much for so many years could no longer care for him because of her disease. Her son also knew she would never give him up, and if and when she went into a home, she couldn't take Elroy with her. So he told her Elroy was very sick and the vet had to put him to sleep.

He telephoned Roelie on October 2, and the next day he and his wife left for Roelie and Tienco's house, with Elroy in their arms.

This is Elroy's story, so I'm going to let him tell it.

The door closed behind them as the people I knew left me in this strange house. I looked up at Roelie and Tienco. They looked like kind people, but they, were strangers. Dachshund tears streamed down my long nose. Scared, I was really scared. I just couldn't stop shaking inside.

Roelie had this big brush and started brushing me. My ears still hurt just thinking about it. In between brushing she talked to me, petted me, hugged me, and gave me all sorts of love, so maybe the brushing could have been worse. Then there were those little treats that mysteriously appeared. I liked that. But I was still scared.

A dish of real dog food was put down in front of me, and it was so good. I don't ever remember tasting anything that delicious. I wasn't even subtle about how I ate. Then I slurped down half the bowl of water. My tummy bulged.

The brushing and combing and grooming kept coming. Next to me was a pile of knots and tangles, all from me. Roelie was persistent, but so very gentle. She knew exactly what a little dachshund liked. She talked to me the whole time, reassuring me, telling me how handsome I was. She even brought out the scissors, and cut some of my long hair away, particularly around my ears.

Then she mentioned "shower" because I smelled so bad.

Me, smell bad? I smelled just fine. I smelled like this for as long as I could remember. It was my smell, my cologne.

A bath didn't sound at all like something I wanted. Wet all over. No, that was more than I could put up with on that first day. Thank goodness, Tienco came to my rescue by suggesting to his wife that they hold off on the washing for a few days.

A quick peak at Tienco made me realize how very sensitive he was to my plight.

I cried into the night and the next day and even some on the following morning. But then something clicked. I liked my new home. I liked Roelie and Tienco, even if they did brush and bathe me.

Roelie at first thought I had epilepsy, I guess, because I was shaking so hard. But with time and regular square meals, the seizures became less and less. Now I don't have seizures anymore.

None of my vaccinations were current either. Roelie took care of that my first week there. The vet checked me thoroughly. He poked me, pushed me, thumped me, and took my temperature, a most embarrassing situation for a dachshund. He squeezed me, looked into my ears, checked my eyes, and jabbed me some more. Then he brought out a huge needle. It was almost as long as I was. Before I knew what had happened, he pricked me with the needle and it was all over. I was up to date with my vaccinations after going without them for at least eight years.

Roelie clutched me tightly telling me what a good boy I was. She hugged me, kissed me, and held me; then we went back to the house.

There was a familiarity here. I had been here before – a long time ago, I just knew it. Besides, I liked those three girls, all long-hair dachshunds who were part of Tienco and Roelie's family. Oh, my gosh! One of them was my mom. That's what I remembered. And my twin sister. She was here, too.

Best of all I get to go outside regularly with the threesome and take care of business. I suspected I was the envy of every dachshund in the neighborhood being with three beautiful lady dachsies, and sometimes a fourth when a wirehaired dachsie named Lotte visited.

No more piddling in the house because no one would let me out. I belonged. I was part of the family. This was my home, my forever home.

Twin sister Iris and a wirehaired visitor named Lotte

Moni (also a rescue dachshund) and Ricky

Chapter 15

An Unexpected Rescue

There are some things dachshunds just live with, whether they live in The Netherlands or elsewhere. Elroy found a naughty little blue parakeet named Ricky who loved to hang from his tail and eat Elroy's food. When it came to Ricky taking a bath in Elroy's water dish, I don't think Elroy had rescue in mind. But I will let him tell you his version of the story.

Ricky used to curl up with all of us dachsies. We really liked him, then he died. So Roelie found another blue parakeet, lighter in color, and named him Ricky after their first bird. We treated him with as much respect as the original Ricky.

But Ricky II was very naughty.

He liked to take baths in our water bowl, and got his beak right in the middle of our food dish. But worst of all, he liked to jump from one to the other of us and swing on our tails—round and round and round he twirls. Can you imagine? A regular three-ring circus trapeze act right in our front room.

My three dachsie ladies and I had enough already. Something had to be done. Not only was it an embarrassment to have a bird swing on our tails, but it hurt when Ricky caught his claws in our fine tail hair.

Our first thought was bird soup, or maybe sautéed parakeet. Not a good idea. Roelie might make us all into hot dogs. We decided not to follow that line of thinking.

Aunt Nancy gave me a dachshund wink. She knew how to open the door leading outside. The door had a wire screen on it to keep Ricky indoors.

One very hot day Tienco unknowingly helped us. He didn't close the main door.

We waited and watched. Roelie and Tienco were entertaining guests. We could hear their laughter. Tienco opened the door for us to go outside, then went back to join the others. Nancy stayed behind.

When no one was looking, she just pushed the screen door open with her nose and stood there holding it long enough for Ricky to pass through. Sure enough, Ricky slipped out with Nancy right behind him. Hopefully, he would fly away and out of our lives. Or maybe the neighbor's cat or possibly a stray one would have parakeet pie.

We would never be blamed, because, after all, Ricky went outside by himself.

Worse luck! He couldn't fly, and all the cats in the neighborhood were snoozing off the heat of the day, well hidden away from our open yard or it would have been good-bye Ricky.

Then he did it. Ricky walked straight to my tail, and started his aerial act going around and around. That's when Tienco saw him through the window, and immediately came out to his rescue.

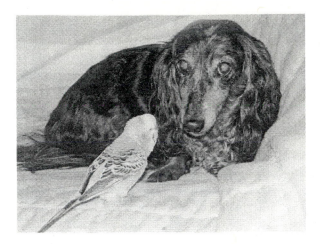

Moni and Ricky

Chapter 16

Scooter Pie the Piebald Dachshund of New York's Subways

I first saw Scooter Pie's picture on the Internet where he was sporting a Sherlock Holmes hat. I sort of wondered if he was hiding a pipe somewhere in the background. And with that nose I knew he didn't need a Sherlock magnifying glass for seeing. His nose would do it all!

But it wasn't always like that. His pet primate told me he was rescued from a horrible puppy mill in Pennsylvania with over 70 dachshunds in little cages. Worse, it's still in operation, and with Pennsylvania as the home state for puppy mills, probably will be in operation for a long time.

Scooter Pie was bought from a Georgia breeder by the Pennsylvania Kennel-from-Hell to breed piebalds. But Scooter Pie had the last laugh. He was sterile, therefore was completely neglected.

This was God's miracle—making him available for adoption.

Scott with Scooter Pie

Scott found him by posting notices that he was looking for an adult piebald dachshund, either a retired breeder or a rescue dachsie. The Pennsylvania Kennel responded.

When Scott got there, he found Scooter completely neglected, with blind dogs, double dapples, puppies—all in little cages and in a mess. Scooter only weighed 9.2 pounds. He was an emaciated skeleton, could not walk on his back legs because he was so malnourished, had torn ears, no fur on his tail, and was non-socialized. Scooter was completely withdrawn, afraid to come near humans. He would hide, and only run out and snatch food when no one was looking.

But now, Scooter Pie is an urban city slicker. He's a bouncy little hound dog, closer to 14 pounds but still thin. He goes to meetings daily with Scott, his urban primate.

Scooter Pie

Both hound and human are from Georgia—two southern farm boys who landed in the Big Apple of Manhattan. Daily meetings, riding the subway, and sitting in meditation groups for an hour when Scott rubs his tummy are all part of his routine. Scooter Pie even has his own dachsie collectibles web site. That's all in a year and a half of love and devotion by his pet primate. Scooter Pie turned five years old this past June. Scooter told me the following tale.

Lazy day for this hound dog. Laid up on the sofa just like a sleepy old bloodhound, taking it easy, enjoying my snooze.

What's that?

Scott putting on his shoes. Dreams quickly scattered, and I begin dancing like a whirlwind. A short jump onto Scott, then another and another. I go round and round keeping him always in the center.

I dive-bomb into my carrying case. Scott looks at me. I look at him. The sherpa bag finds its way right into his hands as we leave the apartment together.

This bag is black, exactly the same size and shape as a gym bag. Its closely-knit mesh on three sides is misleading. The zip-up padded pockets hide a water bowl—hi-tech stainless steel for the New York SoHo Industrial look, of course. Then there's a bottle of Evian, long rawhide chew sticks, extra special "Pupperoni Treats," plastic bags for doggie toilette, and an extension leash. For unsuspecting 42nd Street commuters, my coloring through all that mesh is no more than large white and brown patches passing for wadded-up gym clothes and towel in a gym bag.

On the way to the subway at the Upper Westside we stop at Cloisters Museum and Fort Tryon Park.

The sidewalk is hot when he puts me down. We still have a ways to go to get to the park. Five steps. Sniff at the fire hydrant. Time to sit down. Scott looks at me. I'm exhausted. After all, I was sound asleep when he woke me to go out. I need help. The green is so far away. It's so hot.

Scott picks me up and carries me to the park in his arms, or sometimes in my bag. Its net sides and front for ventilation make it easy for me to see out and know exactly the moment we arrive at the park.

Then it's resurrection for this hound. Dachsie Easter miracle, a la hound doggette!!!

Back to life. I shout out some let-me-down barks. There are squirrels to chase. There's grass to bounce around in. It's cool and soft to my feet. Running, dancing, swirling, my vivid lacquered orange color with gold gilding sets the park ablaze. Scott's right there with my favorite ball. The hot of the day, the gasoline engines from the cars are all behind me. There's a rustle in the nearby trees. Another squirrel.

People laugh. Scott laughs. Then someone asks him if I was the "New York Daily News" celebrity dachshund. Of course. I was chosen for the article on the Dachshund Parade. I led the parade of 500 dachsies. There were only two other piebalds. I gave a dachshund smile, if you know what I mean.

All too soon it's back into my sherpa bag as Scott makes for the subway station.

Once on the subway it's an hour's ride—through Harlem, past Columbia University, Upper West Side, Midtown, and finally we get to the heart of Broadway at the 42nd Street stop, probably the busiest stop in all of New York City. I realize it's time to check out the action, look for any talent scouts, and make my Broadway Debut.

At first it's just my long snout out, the tip first of all to push the "sunroof" unzipped panel back. Then I quickly pop my head up through like a jack-in-the-box, and am usually rewarded by screams, shouts "Oh, my God," and "Lord, I almost had a heart attack." I watch as all those New Yorkers quickly jump up out of their seats to escape the wild animal! That's me.

Amazing that New Yorkers, who can be so jaded, are completely shocked by seeing a DOG IN THE SUBWAY—especially a rare breed, refined piebald dachshund on the subway.

Maybe they think I am an extra-large Manhattan-sized GIANT RAT, because of my long pointy snout, the first part they see. After all, the only kind of common animal New Yorkers are use to seeing in the subway are rats. They eat the garbage along the tracks, and every day you can see them down between the rails.

Just as quickly I disappear back under the sunroof. What anyone looking would see is me calm and distinguished, curled up and chewing on a treat. You know, I can see them the whole time through the net mesh, so I pick my moments—42nd Street with all its cacophony of sounds is my favorite. That's Times Square for all you out-of-towners. After all, you never know when there will be a Broadway talent scout.

Today it's a meditation group. Ah! That means a tummy rub. Scott is so good at that.

Chapter 17

Freddy, Fritz and Bumper

Every Christmas Marilyn received a lot of Christmas greeting cards in the mail. Some of them were even addressed to me, too—Schultz. Many of them came from dachshunds, including Freddy, Fritz, and later, Bumper, all of whom were rescued dachshunds. They belonged to Bertha, who lived in Lindenhurst, New York. That's on the south shore of Long Island. She had polio as a young person; then, many years later, it came back. Of course, I never met these dachshunds or Bertha, and neither has Marilyn. But we enjoyed her letters and the story they told. She wrote that she had eight dachsies over a period of 50 years; all were standards except her current one, Bumper. He is a red tweenie just like me. Well, almost, as I'm not so red.

Freddy belonged to a family. The mother and daughter loved him, but the husband and their son said "absolutely no." They couldn't stand Freddy, as a matter of fact. The decision was made to give him up; Bertha volunteered to take him. He was brought over on a lead. They brought him with a brown bag containing some canned food, kibble, and a little blanket. Everyone left the house except Bertha.

Freddy wandered all over, sniffing and smelling everything, exploring. He finally came back and sat down right next to his big brown bag with the only things he ever owned. His ears drooped. He looked up at Bertha with those big sad brown eyes.

In no time at all Freddy had his own wicker bed, and Bertha made him a nice cushion and special blanket to cover him. Freddy was *happy-go-lucky,* everybody's friend. He lived a very long life full of love and care. Everything was perfect. Well, almost. Then Fritz arrived.

Fritz was a long-haired black-and-tan standard dachshund. He had belonged to a mother and her daughter. The woman had some other kind of dog of her own that she preferred. When Fritz caught fleas, they tied him up to his dog house in the cellar.

The League for Animal Protection (LAP), a local animal rescue group in Ocean Side, New York, heard about Fritz and took him away from that depressing, dreary basement. Then began the job of finding him a forever home.

The group placed him in a foster home with a woman and two little girls, then advertised in the local paper. That's where Bertha found him. Fritz was three years old when he came bounding through the door on a lead. Bertha was in a wheelchair by that time.

Freddy, Bertha's resident dachsie, went right out to greet everyone, including Fritz. After all, they were both black and tan standards, except Freddie had short hair.

Fritz took one look and jumped right on Freddy with every intent of beating him up, eating him alive, finishing him off. I just bet Fritz was remembering that other pampered dog who lived upstairs, while he, Fritzie, was chained to his dog house in the cellar. During that first hour Bertha had to break up two fights, and she told us she had to use force.

She had enough, and I suspect Freddy had already *thrown in the towel.*

"This will never do," she realized, and picked up the phone to call LAP and tell them to come get Fritz.

But something made her hesitate. She said to herself, "I've never given up on any dog, and I'm not about to give up on this one."

Fritz lived for another ten years. But until the day Freddy died, Fritz hated him. Bertha was always on guard. Fortunately, Freddy wasn't a fighter.

From the day the foster home mom transported Fritz to his new home, he walked into Bertha's house and remained beside his new mistress protecting her. He always stayed right next to her wheelchair. He was terrified of floor mops and fly swatters, a sure indication that he had been at the wrong end of them early in his life.

No one ever dare touch Fritz except Bertha. He wouldn't allow it. Bertha was convinced he would bite others, but he never did. She could do anything with him: groom him, comb his long hair and brush his tangles out, clip his nails, clean his ears. Anyone else trying that "would be toast." (Just thinking about getting my nails cut, I know that Fritz must have had a lot of patience to allow her to do that awful thing to him.)

Fritzie's back legs became weaker and weaker as he grew older. Finally, he couldn't stand up any longer. His condition worsened. Bertha bought him a K-9 cart, but Fritzie couldn't use it. The pressure of the cart was on his back, where he had a couple of tumors that wouldn't tolerate the weight. The vet removed one of the tumors but couldn't get the other one. Fritzie's body was just completely worn out. Bertha finally had to make the hardest decision of her life. She had him put to sleep. Fritzie crossed over the Rainbow Bridge where dachsies eventually meet their previous human companions.

After he died, an emptiness settled in. Bertha

wanted another dachshund.

Trudy Kwami, a rescue worker who lived in Brooklyn, found Bumper. He was in a dog shelter and initially went to live with a lady doctor for a month of foster care before he was ready for placement. Trudy heard about Bertha's loneliness, the emptiness of the home in Lindenhurst. She took the time to phone, then transported Bumper to his new forever home with Bertha. Trudy, that year, placed over a hundred dachsies in permanent homes.

How Bumper found his way to the shelter remains unknown. Was he a stray? Did someone put him there? Who knows. But one thing was apparent; he had been a badly abused little hound dog. His left front foot had been broken early in his life. How or why remains a mystery.

Bumper now tops all the dachsies Bertha has ever had. The picture we received last year shows a small pudgy innocent fellow curled up in a ball, sound asleep on the couch. He's a smooth red, quite light in color. When I examined that picture, I realized he was a lot lighter than I am. But underneath all those closely-knit eyebrows for hair, I knew there was a true dachshund spirit.

He likes to play ball. Every morning between 6 and 6:30 he comes in to wake Bertha by sitting and crying until she gets up. Bertha has been training him with hand signals, and Bumper is quick to learn. A teaspoon of peanut butter helps his seizures. She calls Bumper her "mystery" dog.

Watching a brace of Irish setters walk by his house, Bumper fell between an easy chair, end table and radiator and lost his ball. Ouch! He was fine, then suddenly couldn't walk the next day. After two weeks in the hospital, with limited success, he started to take some steps towards recovery. Bertha, her friends, and the vet were all surprised. Restricted to "bed rest," Bumper was put on a diet, lost weight, and is walking

little by little. He's home and has found his ball.
Now Bertha calls him her "miracle" dachshund.

Bumper

Chapter 18

"Animal House"

This tale is strictly about long hairs. It only takes a smidgen of imagination to see who needed to be rescued. My vote goes for all three.

It all begins with a lady doctor, eight legs, two wagging tails and a riot of long auburn hair. As to who had the long hair—well, all three of them did. The trio chewed their way through graduate school with charm. Beethoven and Bismarck concentrated on newspapers, while their owner digested research papers. The entrance of another wagging tail comes later.

Dr. Mary Landers, the starring human in our tail—tale, that is, was a university student working on her dissertation and teaching student seminars. She helped finance her education by serving as housemother in the Delta Tau Delta house at the University of Alabama in Tuscaloosa. One day Mary's brother called her on the phone, offering her a long-hair dachshund puppy as a gift. He thought his sister was lonely. Ha!

Her brother gave her the pick of two, and when she learned Bismarck, the second dachsie, was to be put down because of his pink nose, blue eyes and basic "albino" characteristics, there was no choice at all—she took both of them. Mary took on their mother, Molly, as well, but that happened a little later.

Beethoven became the party animal, the true hound who sat up and begged with no shame at all. Also, he was the cultured one of the two. Beethoven was everyone's friend whether they wanted him to be or not. He liked symphonies, as well as jazz.

Bismarck, on the other hand, was the politically correct southern gentleman. He would patiently sit and wait for treats, and he was very selective in his friendships. He was, first, Mary's personal protector; and only then would he join in the mischief Beethoven had instigated. Bismarck enjoyed looking out the window all day, watching all the people go by.

Mary's best friend often visited, and … oh no, she had a long-hair dachshund named SigmaNu. On those visiting days it was a regular long-hair convention. SigmaNu, a few years older than the two puppies, was designated their godfather and soon became their best friend. He was such a frequent visitor that no matter where the car was parked on "new fraternity row," he knew exactly where the Delt house was and, always excited to visit his buddies and his "Aunt Mary," sprinted directly for it.

Bismarck and Beethoven had two favorite daytime activities—suppers and parties. As to which one took priority, it all depended on the day.

The housemother's suite had two doors, one leading to the foyer of the main house and the second leading directly to the kitchen.

The two cooks working there were the best on campus; right along with all those Delts, both Bismarck and Beethoven appreciated this fact. Wonderful smells always wafted from the kitchen. Both cooks had samples for the dachsie duo, despite Mary's protests. SigmaNu quickly introduced himself to the cooks on his frequent visits. Now the truth comes out; it was the food aromas that led him to the house, and the wonderful tidbits awaiting him once inside with Beethoven and Bismarck.

The main dining room provided even more delectable samples as the fellows quickly succumbed to Beethoven and Bismarck's hungry-hound looks. SigmaNu usually wasn't around for suppertime, but when he was he knew exactly what to do.

Then there were the parties, and all the pretty girls who came in through the foyer. Those times called for an alert eye, not just for the girls, but for their unattended plates of fried chicken and half-filled glasses, soon emptied when the mischievous duo discovered them. Of course, all those young ladies picked the two brothers up and gave them kisses and hugs in between their stolen snacks. (Oh, yes! I'd think I could get used to that kind of life in a hurry.)

Bismarck and Beethoven

The upstairs where the men had their rooms were off limits to girls, but not to Beethoven or Bismarck. They often shot up the stairs to lounge around in the rooms watching TV or listening to the stereo. After all, they thought of themselves as Delts. They were just as wayward as any one of the fellows, and right in the middle of things. Beethoven and Bismarck fit in perfectly.

But life in the fraternity house became too much for the men when another pet arrived. After all, three is a crowd. The university voted "no animals."

Not wanting to lose her job and not wanting to part with Beethoven and Bismarck, Mary rented a "typical" student apartment in one of those old homes in "T-Town" that had been converted into one too many apartments. It was a real dump ... but it was Beethoven and Bismarck's new home. Mary would take turns sleeping one night in the apartment and the next in the fraternity house-mother quarters. Along about then Molly arrived.

Molly

Molly's life had started off with the US Army, well, that is, one service man and his wife from Decatur, Alabama. Molly had been in a pet shop in Frankfurt,

Germany when the couple found her. They later divorced and Mary's brother and sister-in-law ended up with her. Whoops! Another divorce, this time in Molly's new family.

When Mary took Molly in to live with Beethoven and Bismarck, she was about to graduate. That's when they left for a nice apartment building in Decatur.

The wild, hell-raising days in the frat house came to an abrupt end. Life quieted down. Well, sort of. Sometimes the trio lived in Alabama and sometimes on a farm in Tennessee. And Mary added a new rescue dog, an English setter named Lady.

Summers, in southern Alabama, Molly, Beethoven, Bismarck and Lady played havoc with the local sand crabs day and night. They became obsessed with them and continually scratched the door to go out and dig some more.

Their days were spent swimming, surfing, and investigating washed up treasures along the Gulf Coast near Fort Morgan.

Looking for crabs—Beethoven and Lady in surf with Bismarck and Molly checking the sand

Molly had a wayward streak in her as well. One afternoon, while staying in Tennessee, she opened a lunch box and ate the package of cheese curls hiding inside—all while Mary was in a local shop.

When Mary returned to the car, Molly looked all innocent, then hinted that the blame belonged to Bismarck and Beethoven. Mary, not outsmarted this time, soon discovered cheese curls gummed on Molly's teeth. Neither Bismarck nor Beethoven had any such incriminating evidence in their mouths, on their whiskers or anywhere else. Beethoven gave one of his best dachshund smiles. As soon as Mary's back was turned, he pulled out several cheese curls, and down they disappeared.

As he grew into an old man, life in the fraternity house became a mere twinkle in Beethoven's eyes, an almost forgotten memory. His partying days as a young upstart came back to haunt him, however, as aches and pains born of his prodigal days, now meant monthly trips over 60 miles away to the chiropractor. His brother and mother had long since crossed over the Rainbow Bridge.

Beethoven

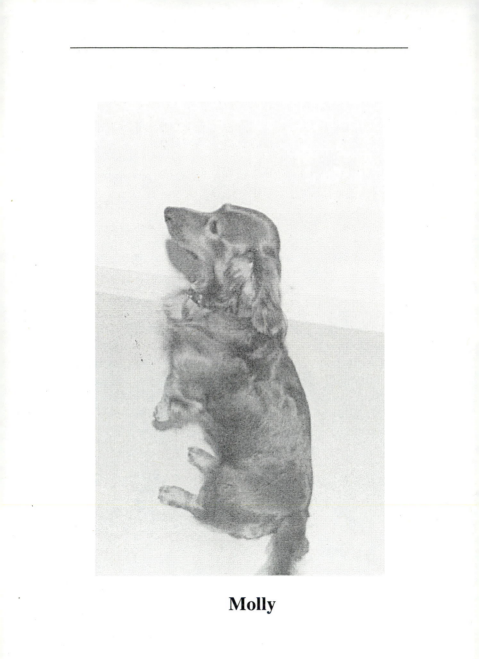

Molly

Chapter 19

Bilingual, at That!

Molly wasn't Mary's only rescued dachshund. Dobie was truly an intercontinental dachshund, and bilingual, understanding both German and English.

A West Point military family whose roots were in Decatur, Alabama, bought Dobie in a pet shop in Munich. They had her for several years, then moved to a new location and could not keep her. So Dobie was flown to the wife's mother living in Decatur.

The older woman was retired and traveled a lot and decided Dobie was spending far too much time boarding in the vet's clinic.

Now Mary had the same vet as the older woman. When Mary lost one of her dachsies, her veterinarian mentioned Dobie. She was beautiful and personable, and, of course, swept Mary right off her feet. Mary refers to dachsies as "little four-legged joys," immediately including Dobie as one of them.

Dobie fast became a favorite of Mary's husband Norman as well. He worked out of town and came home on Fridays. Dobie was always in the driveway to greet him, lavish him with good healthy licks and kiss him. Maybe she was remembering their very special time together in the small nearby town of Cullman, originally settled by Germans, when Norman discovered Dobie's bi-lingual abilities in a little German gift shop. Since I don't know any German, I will let Dobie tell you her story.

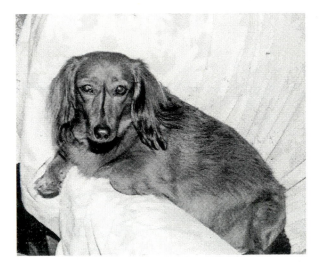

Dobie

Oh, it felt good to have Norman carry me into this little shop. We were in Cullman. Mary stayed home. The heat and the humidity of the South was really bad for my breathing. At home I had to sleep on a down pillow at night. But not all my days were spent being a home body. Often times Norman took me on little outings, and, of course, I had him hold me in his arms most of the time. This was one of those little trips.

Once he put me down on the cool floor I started sniffing around and found a nice little wicker basket. I jumped right in.

A lady came up saying, "Ah, ein typisch Dackel."

Oh my gosh, she spoke German. I barked and jumped back out of the basket. My tail couldn't stop wagging. Then she looked down and laughlingly said,"Frisch genagt ist bald mit Wonnen was gesponnen, flugs zerronnen."

A poet! I barked and barked.

Then she said "Sitz!" I immediately sat down.

Next came "Bleib." I didn't move a muscle, while my dachshund grin went from ear to ear.

"Platz." She pointed to the wicker basket, and I was in it in a flash. Then she pointed to the basket again and said "Pfui. Nicht in Mund nehmen." Of course, I wasn't going to put it in my mouth.

Finally she said, "Such! Norman." Well, Norman wasn't hard to find.

By this time my tail was beating a rhythm against the wooden floor so fast, Norman had to calm me down.

The woman walked over as she was leaving the store, looked right down at me, smiled and said "Auf Wiedersehen."

Dobie not only knew German, she had been trained on command; after all, she was from a military family. There were no leashes for her. She flat out refused wearing one. Mary had to walk Dobie without a leash.

Mary soon learned that Dobie loved old socks. Having been the only child in her previous family, she was always given the discarded ones. Mary didn't know that. Naturally, in her new home Dobie grabbed all the socks she could find. A sockless Mary discovered this one morning when she found Dobie's "toy cache."

There were adjustments to be made, as Dobie was no longer the only dachshund in the family. Initially, there had been two others when Dobie arrived, then Mary and her husband rescued more until there were up to six. Dobie's rigid military upbringing, however, served her well, as she was definitely the dominant one in the household. The others jumped when she barked. Her own four-legged drill team!

Dobie led a privileged life, going on a family

Dobie

vacation 3,000-mile road trip out west with Mary and Norman. In Texas, Dobie never put her feet down on the soil because it was too hot. As I heard the story, I think of the miles I traveled with Marilyn and all those times I had to get out at rest stops. Some of that pavement was hot.

Dobie ran in the hills around Santa Fe, pursued kennels at Carlsbad Caverns, scratched in the white sands of New Mexico, buddied up with UFO's of Roswell, visited her native German-type climate in Ruidoso, New Mexico, skied, shopped and four-wheeled Carson National Forest's Red River, broke bread with Taos Pueblo Indians, and tracked jack rabbits in the desert.

What Dobie enjoyed most, however, despite the heat, was being at home where she lived on the backwaters of the Tennessee River. She was within walking distance of Wheeler National Wildlife Refuge with 35,000 acres to roam. There Great Blue Herons were alarmed by Dobie's intense barking. They flew away in disgust. Muskrats were a favorite; Dobie could swim after them. She had learned how to swim from her faithful friend, Lady, an English setter and also a rescued dog. Of course, these two hunters had to watch out for alligators and water moccasins. Dobie and Lady decided that was Mary's job. They continued to terrorize the muskrats. Neither one saw any of the heavy duty reptiles Mary worried about.

Dobie never forgot her German, however, and looked forward to exploring new haunts with Norman, hoping to one day meet that lady again.

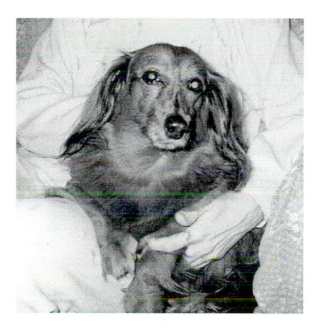

One Very Loved Girl

Chapter 20

Romeo and Juliet

*"**R**omeo, Romeo! wherefore art thou, Romeo?"* Juliet's words rang as clear today as they did in *Shakespeare's time.* Our Juliet was locked up in a tiny kennel in the Broward County Shelter in Fort Lauderdale, Florida. Romeo was several kennels away and out of sight. They had been together for over five years. Then their owners died. Big dachshund tears splashed down on the kennel's cement floor. *"Romeo, come forth; come forth ...."*

It was the week before Christmas. Andy picked up his wife at work.

"Honey, I don't know whether I should tell you this ... I just heard on a public service announcement on the radio. The Broward County Shelter has two red long-hair dachshunds up for adoption. Their owners died, and they have been together for over five years. If a home can't be found for them together, they will have to split them up. What do you think?"

Maggie looked at him and started crying. They just lost their mom, and now they're going to lose each other ... and it's Christmas time (despite the fact that Andy and Maggie were Jewish). We have to keep them together. Give me the phone."

"Whoever gets here first will be accommodated," was the answer. "If someone comes along and only wants one, they will be split up."

Romeo

Juliet

Maggie started yelling at the person over the phone, asking why he had bothered to put the public service announcement on the radio if that was their attitude.

"Lady, just get here first."

It was Friday at 4:30. The shelter was an hour away and it closed at 5:00. They opened again at 9:00 on Saturday.

Andy and Maggie were at the shelter at 8:45 the next morning, a difficult feat for Maggie who admitted she was 15 minutes late for everything in her life, including her own wedding 20 years earlier. Now, she and Andy were the first people "processed," filling out all sorts of papers for adoption. Finally, one of the staff members said he was going into the kennels to bring Romeo and Juliet out so they could meet in a quiet room.

They waited and waited and waited and waited and waited. Finally the staff official emerged from the back with that look you get from people before they give you bad news.

"I'm terribly sorry, Juliet's kennel is empty. She must have been adopted yesterday."

Maggie's temper hit a 7.0 on the Richter scale.

"You idiots. Here we called last night and TOLD YOU we'd be coming. You wanted to keep these dogs together. So do we!" She thought to herself that she was probably in violation of some county ordinance as she continued to rail at the caretaker.

"We schlepped all the way here because YOU wanted a home that would keep these dogs together. That's just great … just great! @#$&%!"

Andy tried to calm Maggie down. They didn't really want to meet Romeo. Why bother? They didn't need more dogs, were only trying to do something for the animals, to give them a good life together and keep them from being split up.

Again the man offered to show them Romeo. He insisted they wait, and sit in a quiet room. He left, promising to be right back.

Maggie looked at Andy. "I think he just wants to get us away from the main area, because we're attracting too much attention."

Andy nodded.

Five minutes later, the same man emerged with two standard red long-hair dachshunds.

"We had never had standards," Maggie said. They look like Irish setters with their legs cut off. Each had a matching red bandanna around its neck."

The official had the biggest smile on his fact. The dachshunds were positively frothing for attention and dove straight for Andy and Maggie's arms.

"When I went to Romeo's kennel to get him, she was in there with him. They were crying for each other all night so they were put together."

The two were covered with fleas and ticks and desperately needed bathing. Romeo had a raging ear infection consisting of multiple bacteria and an evil smell that took a year to clear up. But they had found a home and readily adapted to the other four dachsies living there.

Romeo and Juliet adopted a resident dachsie named Milton as their little boy, but more about Milton in the next chapter. Except to say that once, when the weather got really cold, a rat suddenly appeared in the backyard. Milton was fascinated. He went over to it, and it scratched his snout. Without missing a beat, Romeo bolted over, grabbed that rat in his mouth and clamped down on it. Then he shook it ferociously side to side, until it was quite dead.

Romeo's quick action may have saved Milton from the rat, but a similar incident with a toad could have cost him his life.

Romeo was curious but no match for a Bufo toad, even a small one, let alone the giant he found in the backyard one morning.

If an animal eats the toad or otherwise receives a large quantity of toxin, vomiting, seizures and death may occur in as little as 15 minutes. Even a toad sitting in a dog's watering dish for some time may leave enough toxin to make the pet ill. The death rate for untreated animals exposed to Bufo Marinus, also known as the

Bufo Toad or Cane Toad, is nearly 100% in Florida. Romeo had quite a bit to say about his encounter.

Maggie put all of us out one morning so the kitchen could be cleaned by the housekeeper. Juliet, Estelle, Blanche, Tillie and Milton were all there, along with me. Estelle and I, however, were separate from the others and nosing around in one particularly wet corner where we came upon a huge Bufo toad. It was six or seven inches across, bigger than my head, and I'm a standard, so that's pretty big.

Estelle grabbed it and started poking and prodding. Confronted by Estelle, the toad started secreting bufotoxin from glands on the back of its head in the form of white viscous venom. This milky substance was highly toxic, but I didn't know any better. I took over from Estelle, and started mouthing the thing. My face was dripping Bufo toad goo that oozed everywhere. I looked like I had been "slimed" by the creatures in Ghostbusters by the time I heard Maggie's frantic voice screaming for me.

"Romeo, no...noooooo, no, come!" She had hold of Milton and Blanche, and managed to get them inside the house. Then she came back out for Juliet, still screaming at me to come. When Juliet was pushed indoors, Milton shot through the sliding door. Then Maggie grabbed Tillie and caught Milton again and shoved them both in the door, only to have Juliet come out the sliding door.

She grabbed Estelle and pushed her inside, and Tillie slipped right back out. Next, Maggie had the housekeeper stand by the sliding door, then ran straight towards me, frantically hollering the entire time, and grabbed me. In the house I went, slime and all. Juliet was finally pulled in right behind me.

Maggie was almost out of breath, then switched to automatic pilot, screaming and hollering. Once all six of us were safely indoors, she went into overdrive.

Oh, my gosh! Estelle's head was shoved under the kitchen faucet with cold water running over her mouth and gums, rubbing, splashing water everywhere. The sink was too small.

"No!"

Maggie shot down the steps to the bath below. It had a tub in it. Estelle was not a happy camper when the water was turned on. She bolted, but Maggie had a firm grip. By this time Maggie was huffing and puffing and not gentle at all as she scrubbed.

I was getting squeamish wondering what was coming next.

The housekeeper produced towels, and Estelle disappeared in the folds of a large fluffy one in a flurry of rubbing and drying.

Then Maggie grabbed me. "Okay, Mr. Beefy, it's your turn!"

I'll tell you—not one of my 38 pounds was happy about being shoved into the tub and having my head jammed under a faucet with icy cold water running at full blast. I slithered away and jumped right out of the tub.

That housekeeper was quick, almost as fast as Maggie, as the two wrestled me back into the tub. They almost drowned me. Maggie pried open my mouth with her fingers washing the inside and outside of my gums. I swallowed enough water to launch a battleship. All the time she was pressuring me to stay under the faucet while I pulled away as much as I could choking, sputtering, gasping for air.

Out came another towel. I wanted no more of her care, and ran off into the living room and did laps around the room to stay away from her. I rolled over and over on the carpet just to get dry, and back and forth from the kitchen, through the dining room and into the living room and back again over and over.

Then Maggie examined the others. None of them warranted the treatment Estelle and especially me had received.

I stayed away from Maggie for about 15 minutes, then started licking her hand as she petted me, watching for any signs like twitching, vomiting, shallow breathing that would mean a sudden flight to the local emergency vet. She had done a good job of cleaning the milky secretion from both Estelle and me. No such signs appeared.

"Romeo. Courage, man; the hurt cannot be much." Juliet gave me a dachshund smile as she curled up in the corner and fell fast asleep.

"It's okay, Mom." I realized then how scared Maggie was and only trying to protect me. Estelle, however, was far less forgiving and wouldn't have a thing to do with Maggie for the rest of the morning.

No more free excursions to the backyard. Either Maggie or Andy stood guard against the monster Bufo. There were no return performances, and eventually we were allowed unfettered access to the yard without parental control. Maggie still checks out the yard though before opening the sliding doors, just scanning for the ugly little beasts.

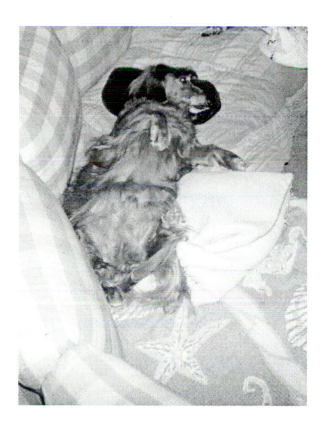

Romeo

Chapter 21

Ten Pounds of Trouble

Milton's story is a sad one with a very happy ending. He was rescued from a puppy mill where someone thought it would be cute to cut off his tail and beat him. Good grief! His little stump of a tail and several marks on his coat were the only visible signs. Emotionally, there was other evidence.

Originally, Milton had been called Baron von something or other but was soon renamed. Andy had a client in Pompano Beach, Florida, who knew Maggie and Andy were "crazy about dachshunds." She rescued Milton and called the couple up, and that was that. They took him.

Milton trained under Romeo to be an alpha dog, and assumed the role of "King." Andy fell in love with him, and now has the son he always wanted.

Milton Theodore Kassier is a handful. It's lucky for him that he was so cute, or Maggie probably would have killed him. She describes him as "ten pounds of trouble."

Now I wonder why such a little cutie would be so much trouble. The answers come in a flash. When they try to bathe him, clean his eyes, cut his nails or give him medication, he becomes a canine eel. He slithers and slinks, rocks and rolls until he gets away. And he does get away. His behavior is probably because of the abuse he suffered before he came to Andy and Maggie's home.

Those first few weeks he was a very quiet and shy dachshund. He wouldn't lick. Andy and Maggie were "licky" people and expected licks from their dogs. In exchange, their four-footed family received endless supplies of jerky treats. Perplexed. Why not? All dachsies enjoy sneaking in a lick or two or three or four or more. But not Milton.

One evening Andy's face lit up in a smile. He disappeared into the kitchen and emerged with a jar of crunchy peanut butter. Oh, the best kind—my favorite. He dotted his face in about twenty spots with peanut butter, so it looked as if he had a bad case of the peanut butter measles. Then he lay down on the floor, and waited for the inevitable to happen.

Milton couldn't resist a peanut, even crunched up ones. He started at the forehead and worked his way right down to the chin, licking madly until Andy's face was sparkly clean. He has been giving kisses every since that day, and is the "lickiest" of all their fur babies.

Milton is no longer the shy little dachsie that first came into Maggie and Andy's life. He is one expressive hound. His whine sounds almost like a baby's cry for attention, for milk, for, of course, peanuts when his K-9 nose detects one in a shirt pocket. When the can opener is taken from the drawer in the food room, that's a translation for "kitchen," that means "wet food, oh boy!" Milton is up on the lower cabinets and whines more.

The sensation of touch is something Milton really likes. He is deliberate in his attempts to get some belly and chest rubs. His first move is to jump up on the lap, then sit up on hind legs and start scratching with one of his front paws. A quick maneuver onto his back follows with both front paws close together motioning—he's ready. He doesn't stop until the moment he's touched on his chest, neck, ears, or anywhere (it doesn't really matter), then he starts right up if the touching or petting stops.

If he really wants attention and someone doesn't respond in an appropriate manner, he will pull his paws over his snout, start at his eyes and move his paws down to the tip of his nose. Or, he will bite the nose in front of him—not his, his pet primate's.

Now Milton believes in marking his territory and is so bad he has inherited the name, "Milton, Destroyer of Homes." No matter how many times Maggie lets the little "devil" out in the yard, he always saves a few drops to mark his favorite spots in the house. Two separate housekeepers in broken English complained "it smells" about the carpets, and that's when Maggie had enough.

One long day about a year ago Milton was an exceptionally bad boy. Some food had been left on the table, and, of course, Milton managed to jump up on the chairs at the kitchen table and get to the food. Oh yes, he knocked a few things on to the floor. The result: a mess! Maggie then caught him peeing in the house that night after cleaning up his earlier demolition. That did it.

Maggie and Andy were together with him in the bedroom, picked him up and put him on the bed. A scolding followed by a swat on the butt—and there was no reaction. Another tiny swat, and nothing—total "flat affect."

Both simultaneously realized at the same moment, "Oh, my God ...." They understood how badly Milton must have been abused in his previous life. Not even a flinch when he was tapped on his rump. They picked him up and hugged and hugged him and kissed him madly. And vowed never to strike him again.

Milton wedged himself between Andy and the pillows, burrowed under a blanket. Like an ostrich, he left only his heart-shaped "tush" exposed (so called because there is a patch of blond hair on his behind, surrounded by chocolate brown, in the shape of a heart) and fell fast asleep, knowing he had now gained full control of his primates, and his peeing.

All Ten Pounds of Milton

Chapter 22

Becky Jo's Great Adventure

Another night on the computer, another story, only this time it was about a lovely long-hair sable red female dachshund. My ears definitely picked up upon hearing about a "beautiful lady." Sable red—my favorite color.

Becky Jo lived in Gresham, Oregon, not far away from Portland. She was two years old and in heat. Her perfume was driving her human mom Carol's two male dachshunds crazy. But Carol wasn't about to let those two mate with Becky Jo—no way, Jose! So she had to do something and do it quick.

November is a cold and stormy month, and that November ten years ago was no different from previous years.

Carol crated up Becky Jo one night and took her to the Mount Hood Dachshund Club for their monthly meeting. Carol's friend Kati, then eight months pregnant, met her there and agreed to keep Becky Jo for the remaining time she was in season—three weeks.

Rain continued to pour down as the two women hurriedly loaded the crate and Becky Jo into Kati's car. Kati's two-year-old daughter was there as well, adding a bit of confusion. Everything outside was wet and muddy and gooey. Ugh! Not a friendly evening.

Kati took off for her 20-acre farm in Corbett near Larch Mountain, a good five miles away from the Vista House where visitors stopped during the summer months to view the Columbia River Gorge. During the winter it was basically abandoned, and so was the road pretty much except by locals. Carol went home much relieved after the dachshund club meeting knowing Becky Jo was in safe hands and away from male dogs.

Sheets of rain streamed down the windshield as Kati drove home. The wind swirled around the car, rocking it now and then as it headed for the farm.

Once there Kati rushed her daughter into the house, leaving the car door open, then dashed back for Becky Jo. A flash of lightning lit up the drive. Rolling peals of thunder followed a few seconds later, adding to the nastiness of the night.

Kati peered into the car only to find the crate's door open.

Empty car! Empty crate! Magic—Houdini at his finest. Disappearing dog act. Pull the dachshund out of the hat. What! No magician's hat? Worse yet, no Becky Jo. The crate was empty. The latch hadn't been fully fastened. Now the door stood wide open.

"Becky Jo, come on girl. Come on. Becky Jo! Becky Jo!" Kati hollered, then panic set in. "Becky Jo! Becky Jo!" And then anger at not getting a response, "Becky Jo, come here this minute."

The wind twisted Kati's words, mixing them up with the now frightening sound of torrential rain. No barks. No Becky Jo. Nothing except the howling gale.

Kati didn't call Carol. She couldn't. Minutes ticked away turning into hours. In desperation, Kati put food out, safe from the tempest but right where a little dog could find it. How could she tell her friend that she, Kati, had lost her prize dachshund.

More time passed intermingled with calls outside. "Becky Jo, come on girl, please come."

Exhausted, she couldn't stay awake any longer. She would have to go to bed and look for Becky Jo in the morning when it was light. She'll find her then. But she didn't.

All the next day Carol felt uneasy at work. Something was wrong. She just knew it.

She grabbed the phone and finally called Kati. A worm of fear turned inside Carol's stomach. Tears flowed between the words as Kati told her what happened. The food left out was gone.

Carol's right hand flew to her heart, and in some sickening subdivision of a second, her mouth went dry, her throat closed, and sweat broke out from the crown of her head to her toes. Almost as quickly, a desperate hope bloomed in her brain. A dog had been there, after all—maybe it was Becky Jo.

Or, had some other animal had a morning feast? Had some stray male dog found Becky Jo? No answers.

Kati's husband Clint had called and called searching all over the acreage. No Becky Jo. But Becky Jo didn't know Clint; she wouldn't come to him anyway.

Maybe Carol's voice would entice Becky Jo from her hiding place, that is, if she were still alive. Carol all but flew over to Kati's house in her car. She called and hollered and yelled and begged. She tramped through the wet woods, sloshed through the open fields. Night found her in tears pleading, making promises, praying. No Becky Jo.

"Becky Jo, come on girl. Becky Jo." Her voice rang in desperation. Panic was just one layer beneath the surface.

Her heart pushed against her throat. The heaviness in her footsteps told it all.

The panic that lived beneath Carol's skin burned through to the surface, paralyzing her where she stood. Her chin began to quiver. She tried to scream, but no sound came to her throat.

"We'll find her," Kati promised.

The temporary paralysis finally broke, and Carol jerked as though she had taken a blow. "Becky Jo!" she screamed. "Come to me!" Tears flooded down her face.

Signs were posted on the road, and distributed in the local shops. Notices were out. Pictures of Becky Jo were attached.

Larch Mountain was a known hangout for cougars, those large 140-200 pound cats that would have a dachshund in a twitch of a whisker. Becky Jo would make a nice hors d'oeuvre.

What! There was a sighting. "A little long-haired red-sable dachshund. You know, one of those long, low-to-the-ground wiener dogs. Saw it up by the junction."

A race to the junction proved fruitless, as there was no Becky Jo.

Another sighting, and another and another, and every one leading towards Larch Mountain. Becky Jo was on the move. She continued her elusive trail well ahead of her pursuers. Several nights passed. Becky Jo was always just ahead of Carol.

Kati handled the phone. After all, she was eight months pregnant and couldn't go tramping through the woods, and she wasn't working. But she could help by answering the phone, keeping a portable one with her.

The radio was on. The announcer advertised a "pet psychic." That's it! A pet psychic, Kati dialed the number given and described Becky Jo. She told her all she knew.

The woman listened. She said she could see Becky Jo. "She is alive, but very hungry." Then she described the area in detail where she believed Becky Jo to be.

Clint drove directly to the spot, to where she had placed the dachshund. There was evidence of a small dog having been there, but no Becky Jo.

The psychic continued to be involved.

"I can see her. She's cold and hungry. She's crying and scared." More landmarks were given and they were leading towards Larch Mountain and Crown Point's

Vista House, empty during the winter months.

Clint checked. More evidence—this time long red-sable hairs caught on a bush. A dog had been there. Was it Becky Jo? Clint returned home downcast at not having found her.

The psychic continued—"She is still alive, but she's so hungry. There are some railroad tracks and a large body of water nearby. She is very scared. Something's after her."

The phone rang. "Lady, I spotted your dog walking down the middle of the highway towards Crown Point just minutes ago."

Kati's husband dashed out the door and gave his motorcycle a good hard pump as he started it. He was determined. He was going to get that dachshund this time. That low-to-the-ground girl wasn't going to escape him. No, not this time.

The old Crown Point Highway had rock walls of stone and mortar acting as barriers for motorists and lead right up to the Vista House. The lower rock walls had been there since 1913, and the stone wall around the parking area since 1916 when the Vista House had been built. Every so often there was a little round hole in the wall for the rainwater to escape.

It was along this section of highway that Clint spotted Becky Jo.

"Now I've got you, you little sausage hound."

He slammed on the brakes, propped his cycle up on its stand and darted after Becky Jo. She saw him coming and quickly split off the highway diving through one of the rainwater spouts and fell straight down a 30-foot embankment.

Clint, not knowing about the drop on the other side, leapt over the wall right after her, tumbling down the steep grade head over heels. Gravel cut him. He kept falling.

Yells unfit for a little dachshund's ears echoed up the cliff. Gravel and rocks were still sliding. Then silence. Clint stood up, miraculously with no broken bones, just bruises, scratches and cuts. Mud caked his clothes. The breath knocked out of him, and weak, he looked around to get his bearings.

You're wondering what happened. Marilyn and I drove down to Vancouver, Washington, where Becky Jo and Carol now live. I asked Becky Jo to tell the end of her story. She had just turned 12 years old on her last birthday, and was a great grandmother to boot. And, oh my, she was still a knockout. She stole my breath away, then proceeded to tell her story.

Cold dog. Tired. Hungry, so hungry. Those little tiny mushrooms I found didn't go very far. Neither did the berries. Miserable day. A creepy mistiness spread through the woods, circling everything in its path. Decaying leaves, dank, dark, and wet moss, everywhere. The rotting stench was overpowering.

I shook from my nose to the tip of my tail the way dachshunds do. I had been running since late yesterday afternoon, ever since I heard the cougar's growls in those rocks.

I stumbled across a large piece of bark from a fallen tree. Inside its cavity was a cache of fresh, cold rainwater. I drank deeply, feeling slightly better. Dead and fallen fir boughs provided a comfortable bed. I lay down just for a few moments.

When I woke up the cougar's growls were still in my head. I must be dreaming. Mist and fog everywhere. Then far away I heard the cougar scream. The unearthly sound slammed against my ears and reverberated through the forest. I scrambled up, not even looking. Ouch! I smacked right into another thorny bush.

Sharp stickers added to my collection of burrs embedded in the long hairs on my ears and tail. I didn't stop to pull them out. The wind made the trees creak and moan. Then another scream. Murkiness settled around me. I ran.

The fog started to dissipate. Sunlight filtered down through the trees and sideways across the woods. The sun had finally burned through the fog. I must have slept a long time. There was a clearing ahead.

Bird calls echoed through the small clearing, punctuated by the rapid fire "pock-pock-pock" of a woodpecker, and two gray squirrels looking for seedpods chased each other through the upper branches of the cottonwoods.

More light. The clearing turned out to be a road, the old Crown Point Highway with its rock barriers along the side. I stepped right out onto the cement and started walking down its center. No more bushes hit me in the face. No more trees behind in which all manner of monsters hid.

The animals fell silent. A new sound had entered the woods. A motor. An old one, its valves tapping from unleaded gasoline. The noise grew steadily until the green hood of a pickup truck broke from the far curve ahead of me into the dappled sunlight.

The pickup truck was almost on me when I saw it. I ducked to the side of the roadway and out of its way. The driver slowed down looking at me carefully, then sped on. The engine soon died away.

I followed the yellow line down the highway's center. Fog all gone. I wanted a drink of water. So thirsty after walking so far. No more cougar screams.

I heard the screech of brakes behind me. A big man jumped off his motorcycle and was running right for me.

"Becky Jo."

No, I didn't know him. I had never seen him before in my life.

I shot through the little hole in the nearby rock wall and out the other side only to find myself rolling down a huge cliff, out of control, sliding, sliding all the way to the bottom.

I looked back in time to see that big man jump over

the wall behind me, then tumble as he flew through the air and down the same embankment where I had just fallen. I didn't wait for him to get to the bottom.

I dove under a bush, up a small grade and dashed into some more thorny shrubs.

His yells were well behind me when I abruptly came face to face with another animal, menacing, and slightly smaller than me. She was dark brown except for a white spot below each ear. Then I took a look at her incisors. No, no, no. I knew I didn't want to tangle with her.

A flat and wide head with a nose slightly arched, she gazed at me. Her thick, heavy body was covered with coarse, dull fur. She took in my scent, then started walking right towards me grinding her teeth. She came a step at a time, slowly, ever so slowly, but never really hesitating. Whistles and booming sounds emitted from her throat. A squeal followed, and more grinding noises with her teeth.

Oh, my gosh. I started barking, and kept right on barking.

Quiet unexpectedly, something grabbed me from behind. I twisted and turned, then bit the grabbing thing. Oops! It was the big man, and now he was angry with me. I wiggled and squealed, and screamed and barked. All to no avail. He had snuck up to me, afraid I'd run. His hold, now that he had me, was nothing less than a vise grip. I couldn't move. Carefully he climbed back up the grade. No way was he going to let me go. I squirmed and nipped at his hands, but he was firm and resolute. He held on.

"You found her." A friend of his commented who happened upon the scene in a golf cart.

"And none too soon—one of the biggest mountain beavers I've ever seen had her cornered. I scared it off, but even then it snarled at me."

"Must have a nest nearby. They usually aren't that aggressive."

He held me tight, while his friend started up the golf

cart motor. *I didn't like the noise but I couldn't do a thing about it.*

Clint took a moment looking down at the railroad tracks far below and the large body of water, the Columbia River. He held me even tighter just shaking his head. I thought I was going to pop.

Kati met us after a quick and very breezy ride back to the farm. Clint and his friend turned around in the golf cart and went back for the motorcycle, and Kati started scrubbing me, first working those nasty burrs out of my coat, then dunking me in a washtub full of warm soapy water. This was followed by a dousing of clean water. A quick towel rub, more combing, and, of course, some of my favorite food.

A car door slammed outside. I looked up just in time to see Carol race through the kitchen's open door. Dachshund tears of joy streamed down my nose as she picked me up. I snuggled deep into her protective arms. I couldn't give her enough kisses, and I squealed and squealed as she held me crying. It was one wet reunion.

No, I didn't get pregnant on my great adventure. I didn't even see another dog.

Three Generations: Gracie (Granddaughter), Libby Jean (Daughter) and Becky Jo (at age 12)

Chapter 23

It's Best to Let Sleeping Bears Lie

Nicky was a middle-aged, brown, wirehaired dachshund when Marilyn first met him in King Salmon, Alaska. The wrong place for a dachshund if you ask me. Worse off, there are no veterinarians in King Salmon. The closest one was in Anchorage, some 300 air miles away. His owners Terry and Kathy were very proud of him. Not having known a wirehaired dachshund before, Marilyn found him intriguing.

His hair was thin along his back; that's why he had a little snow suit for going out during the cold time of the year. Along his shoulder blades there were two mean-looking scars. And that leads to his story.

"Nicky," a man's voice called.

It happened on one of those hot, lazy summer days. I went outside sniffing around. Kathy's dad was visiting Terry and Kathy.

He called me again. Seeing me, he threw a ball. I gave chase, grabbed it and held onto it for a while, then I let him have it again. He threw it once more, only

112

further this time. I dashed into the bushes, but before I picked it up, I caught an unmistakable whiff of something I hadn't smelled before.

I forgot the ball and looked around, trying to determine just where that odor was coming from. I walked into the scrub willows next to our house. They were not any taller than Terry, but to me it was a forest. The leaves were all yellows and reds.

There it was again. A musty smell clung to the branches. The air was charged with a foul odor. I darted right for it. The stench was overwhelming. No detour. No caution. Just remove that intruder off my property.

The nearby limbs crackled. I shuffled through the dry leaves under my feet. A blade of grass smacked me in the face. I was almost on that stench, and ready to attack, when...

Whoosh!

Ouch!

My back smarted from pain I had never felt before. My shoulders hurt.

I looked up to find myself eyeball to eyeball with a nasty-tempered bear, and well within his reach as he stood up shaking the sleep from his fiery eyes. He had done the swiping at me while still napping.

I didn't wait for him to fully wake up, but shot back through the trees and into my front yard, howling. Blood marked all fifteen yards of my trail.

Kathy's dad saw me first, yelled for Kathy, then ran to me. He looked up in time to see a big brown hulk head out the other side of the brush and down the driveway.

"My gosh! It's a bear!"

"Bear!"

Kathy dashed out of the house, grabbed me, picked me up. Red oozed from my shoulders. A whimper escaped.

My back hurt. It was like a thousand bees had

simultaneously stung me all in the same spot. Two of the bear's claws had ripped open my back. Gore was everywhere and dripped all over Kathy. I whimpered again, then screamed. She took me into the house, at wit's end as to what to do.

"The closest vet is in Anchorage. He'll bleed to death before we get him there," Kathy cried to her dad. Then she suddenly said something about Dick, a state worker who was always patching up his black hunting labs.

"That's it," she half cried loudly. She grabbed the phone, opened the telephone book at the same time holding me and praying.

"Dick come quick. It's Nicky, he's been attacked by a bear. Can you stitch him up?"

Kathy held me so gently, but oh, it hurt. I was howling and crying and scared. My shoulder stiffened. Every time I moved, it hurt more.

Dick walked in minutes later, took one look at me and said, "Oh, my God!"

Everything was spinning. I felt awful. Kathy was there. She still had hold of me. I felt safe in her arms.

"All my dogs are eight-ten times his size. I have no idea what kind of a dose to give him to put him out without killing him. And, he needs a tetanus shot to boot."

"You've got to do something. His whole back is ripped open."

Then everything went black.

Much later I woke up, my hair was cut away all along my back and I had two rows of stitches right where the bear had swiped. Groggy, I tried to stand, but fell immediately. And, so thirsty. I'd give anything for just a little drink of water.

Kathy held me and kept me from falling. I didn't try to fight anymore. I just lay there.

Over the next few weeks Kathy put neosporin on my back, irrigated the wound to let it heal from the inside

114

out, and watched me every minute. I wasn't going anywhere. I hurt everywhere, and my back felt as if red hot pokers were attached. I couldn't get at it to bite those stitches out.

I didn't play ball for quite a while after that.

I vowed then and there I'd get that bear. Imagine hiding in my yard, then attacking me!

Chapter 24

Snoopy Never Waited for Groundhog Day

This is another one of those stories Marilyn heard from teachers while working in Alaska. This time it was about a dachsie from Missouri. One woman, Shirley, said that her parents' dachsie, Snoopy, spent a lifetime of being rescued by her parents. They never failed him. Sometimes Shirley and her two boys helped find him.

Snoopy was a brown, smooth hair dachshund who grew up in Missouri's Ozark hills. He initially arrived as a Christmas present from Shirley and the boys because he was little and could do well in her parents' 50-foot trailer. But when they moved back to the farm, Snoopy spent his summers chasing groundhogs on their 258 acres.

He would disappear for days at a time. Desperate, Shirley and her two sons were called to help find him. The three of them and her dad would tramp all over the land hoping to hear Snoopy bark so they could get him out of a groundhog burrow. They were afraid he'd stay underground until he died. Snoopy knew a good thing when he saw it; every groundhog only acted as another enticement for his next adventure.

"Snoopy!" *"Snooooooopy, come on, Snoooooopy! Please come. Come on Snoopy!"*

That was Shirley. She sounded far away, but I could hear concern in her voice. Maybe even desperation. But then, there was that musty fur smell. It couldn't be more than a few feet ahead of me.

My front paws started going faster, just another couple of feet. That's all I had to dig, but then the fur started digging as well. I could hear him. I stopped a moment. Yes, the smell was still there, and so was his digging and he was getting away from me. No, I wasn't going to let that happen.

More dirt flew past my feet and dropped somewhere behind my tail. I let out a yip, followed by two short barks.

"Snoopy!" *Shirley called, "I've found him!"*

This time the voice was much closer, and it was one of the boys. "Here, right here!"

Then I heard dad come running over. I kept digging, I wanted him to know where the fur was, where I wanted him to dig. I bit into the soil. Dirt, roots and a few stray pieces of grass clung to the inside of my mouth. Another bite. Tired as I was, my front paws were going with renewed effort. Dirt flew behind me.

Barking now, I continued to inch forward. The hole was there, it just needed expanding for me to get down to the fur.

Then I heard it, the long tool dad carried with him. I could tell from the sounds in the soft dirt above me that dad was screwing it down into a new hole just ahead of me, just where the fur was.

"I've got it" *dad declared triumphantly.*

I looked up and could see sky through the hole dad made.

Up the newly-made hole I sprang, but I didn't quite reach the top. I was tired from days of work going after that fur.

"Come on, Snoopy," Shirley called. "You can do it."

I thought about the fur. This time I jumped a little harder, clawing at the top of the hole.

Dad hit the fur just once with his little club and tossed it in my direction. My tiredness all but forgotten, I lunged, attacked from all sides, growled, and shook it until there was no more life left in the fur.

By this time Shirley came running, picked me up and started back through the field.

"Look how thin he is" Shirley said.

"Well, after two nights digging you'd be skinny too!" Dad responded.

Several small cedars had sprouted this past spring just where I had first found the hole and followed the smell down into the earth. Dad clipped them off as he went by.

"Got to get this planted next year, before the cedars take over." Dad led the walk home.

Shirley, and her two boys followed. We headed for the edge of the field where a small stand of mammoth oaks shaded the way. Just beyond was a rocky bluff. The summer day was soft and warm. The heat above ground felt good after my hours of tunneling. Along with it, however, came a tingling all over my skin.

Every part of me itched. I started nipping until I caused a little red spot before Shirley caught me.

"No!"

She held my paws so I couldn't bite them anymore. The rawness hurt. I wanted to get at it.

Ticks and chiggers, that's what the Ozarks had, and, of course, groundhogs, but one less after this morning. I twisted and turned. If I could just pull some of those ticks out. I didn't mind the dirt in that hole; some of it still stuck around my teeth along with a weed or two. But underground there were also the ticks, hordes of them.

I yipped.

118

Shirley put me down but kept a watchful eye on me. Her older boy was right behind me. I knew he could catch me if he had to, so I followed along at least for the moment. Besides, Shirley's comments about my weight loss brought on pangs of hunger.

A half hour later, we came to the house.

"Where did you find Snoopy this time?" Mom asked dad.

"Up in the field near that stand of old oaks."

"Why that's more than a mile away. Good thing Shirley and the boys were home, or you'd never have found him this time. Stomping around every foot of this land just for that fool dog ...," and she shook her head.

Then she added, with a twinkle in her eye, "Did he get the groundhog?"

"Yep!" He paused, then said, "Now ma, you love him as much as anybody and besides it's born in him to hunt."

"I know, but every time he doesn't come home, you have to call Shirley and the boys to walk all over the ground hoping you'll hear his bark somewhere in one of them tunnels. One of these days, you won't find him."

"Oh, Snoopy, he would come back, eventually."

"I don't think so; he'd just die down there waiting for that groundhog."

Shirley returned from the kitchen with a bowl of my favorite food. Between scratching and eating, things definitely improved.

Mom didn't say anymore, just shook her head. Then dad came over with some matches and started hunting all over for ticks. He heated up a small iron and when he found a tick he branded it, causing it to back right out of my skin. I didn't move too much, because I knew the feel of his hot iron on my skin was something I didn't want.

Next came a bath. It eased some of the rawness. Those little red spots of blood soon disappeared in the water. The strong bar of soap would have been enough *to kill any old ticks, but worse luck, I smelled just like that bar of soap.*

"Dad, you're not letting him out again?' This time it was Shirley.

"Oh, if I know Snoopy he won't take off for a few days."

I rolled in the grass, just for that earth smell, then headed for my basket right at the foot of dad's big rocker on the porch. My pillow was right where I left it. Scratching, I turned around several times to get it just right, scratched again, then curled up in a ball.

The sun beat down on my back. A few mosquitoes buzzed overhead. There were grasshoppers down at the bottom of the steps. Right now they didn't interest me as my tummy was full, besides, Shirley was right there, and she never let me eat those grasshoppers. I looked out over the pond in front of the house. The rowboat bobbing up and down became one with the sun. The voices of my family sitting on the porch talking about the day began fading away. My eyelids grew heavier and heavier; they just wouldn't stay open. My nose twitched. The fields rose around me as I followed that musty fur scent somewhere up ahead.

"Ma, do you think dogs dream?"

"I guess so. Just look at Snoopy's feet go right now."

Chapter 25

Eiger's Home!

Benz wrote me a note the other day saying I needed a long-hair dachsie for a companion.

While I love chasing Marilyn's three cats around the house, having another fellow for a brother would be special. Marilyn realized this when we visited Becky Jo's family of long hairs. Seven all at once was a bit much, but I soon lost my bashfulness and started frolicking on the floor with all those girls and boys, including Becky Jo and a corgi named Jasmine.

Then Marilyn read on the internet,

Have to make a heartbreaking part with my two-year old dachshund. I am moving to New Zealand and can't take him with me. He is a beautiful little dog, 12 pounds, black and tan. He is called a tweenie. Just between a standard and a mini. He loves other dogs, especially little ones. He is a very faithful dog. A little uncertain of strangers at first, but an absolute doll when he gets to know you. He is potty trained and has the perfect amount of energy. He would be a good dog for a couple or elderly person. He hasn't been around children, but I think would be fine, also good with cats. He is my baby, and it is important that he goes to a good home. Can send pictures as well.

Marilyn telephoned. We jumped in the car the next day and drove to Oakland, California. Fourteen hours later, along came Eiger, and sat down beside her. Marilyn said yes, and I said okay.

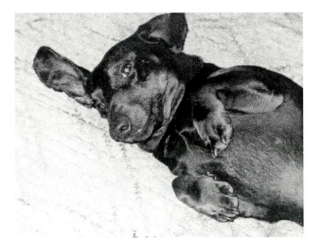

A new baby brother, Eiger is almost two-and-a-half years old. Described as a black-and-tan, 12-pound smooth, he weighs in at 17 pounds-4-and-half ounces.

Take the "T" out of Tiger, add an "E" and you have Eiger, named for "The Eiger," a famous climbing wall in the Austrian Alps. Yes, he likes to climb. No one knows exactly how old Eiger is, but he was about four months of age almost two years ago when he was found lost and roaming around Golden Gate Park in San Francisco. He was taken to a shelter and placed in a home in Oakland. So he's a double rescue, and well adjusted for all that.

And, oh, yes, he's shown more interest in the cats than they would like to admit.

Eiger

He has one little problem; he keeps showing his little red rocket, can't keep it tucked away. Everything was all dried out. The vet gave Marilyn some lubricant, and instructions, and he's doing much better. Personally, I think it's his way of getting attention.

Eiger, not used to all this book writing, made a few comments after spending almost 14 hours sitting on Marilyn's lap as she drove home from Oakland to Vashon Island with me sleeping next to her. I managed to sneak up onto her shoulders for about an hour.

I like riding in cars, and Marilyn's car has the cutest little red button in between the seats. Every time I jump over to her side when she leaves, I usually step right in the middle of it, and instantaneously there are lights flashing green on the dashboard. I wonder what that is? Schultz just rolled his eyes.

I realized with Eiger's words that I would escape blame for stepping on the emergency light switch in the future, at least, some of the time. I gave my best dachshund grin.

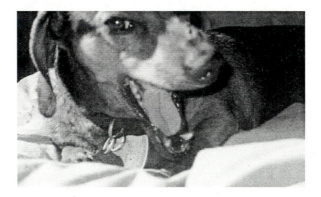

Schultzie

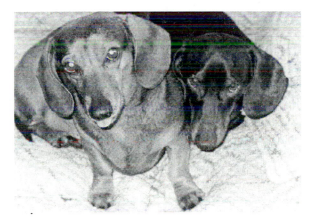

Eiger and Schultz

Author's Note

These are the top five rescue groups that I have come across. I have listed them here for the benefit of any of my readers who decide they want a rescue dachshund. All are non-profit organizations.

PETFINDER ((www.Petfinder.com)
The "Grand Central" clearing house site for rescue/animal shelters, with pet search engine—select "Dachshund" in breed, put in your zip code in the search form on the site. I would suggest doing a NATIONAL search, as some dogs are listed under the state location of the rescue organization, which may have dogs in many states across the USA. There is also a bulletin/message board. This would be my first stop when looking for a dachshund. Many of the other dachshund rescue organizations list their dachshunds here. Photos of dachshunds are posted once you get to an individual organization.

DACHSHUND RESCUE OF NORTH AMERICA
(www.drna.org)
National Dachshund Rescue web page that has photos of dachshunds, and contact information for local rescue groups. Search by state. This is probably the largest dachshund-specific site.

COAST TO COAST DACHSHUND RESCUE
(www.C2CDR.org)
This is a national non-profit, all-volunteer organization dedicated to rescuing needy dachshunds and dachshund mixes. CCDR strives to find homeless dachshund-loving forever families all over the US and Canada. Includes photos of dachshunds.

DARE TO RESCUE DACHSHUND RESCUE
(www.DareToRescue.com)
This is another smaller national dachshund rescue web page. There are photos of dachshunds.

ALMOST HOME DACHSHUND RESCUE
(www.almosthomerescue.org)
This is a network of independent rescue volunteers who work together to rescue abandoned, abused, and unwanted dachshunds. AHDRS is a non-profit organization. Photos of dachshunds are included.

I am also adding the **DISABLED DACHSHUND SOCIETY** (www.rushmore.com) to this list as well. They are located at 830 State Street, Spearfish, South Dakota 57783. This group is dedicated to helping disabled dachshunds that would otherwise be euthanized prematurely either due to the lack of knowledge on the part of the owner, or because it is not financially viable for the owner to invest in the treatment and care of the disabled dog.

REPUTABLE BREEDERS
The reputable breeder is someone who knows the breed, understands the breed standard, and breeds dogs that have something to contribute to improve the breed, usually dogs that have been shown and achieved championship status.

A reputable breeder will also only sell a puppy with a contract, which states that if the buyer can't keep the dog, it goes back to the breeder. That's because the breeder wants to always know where his/her puppies are! Circumstances can change where a person can no longer keep a dog. Some of these situations were touched on in the stories told.

Any reputable breeder will NOT sell to a pet shop. So if you want a puppy, and know now that you should not buy from a pet store, where do you go? If you want a purebred, there are many reputable breeders for every breed imaginable that will sell you a quality, healthy puppy costing much less than a pet-shop dachshund. Contact the national breed organization for references.

Purebred dogs are not necessarily better pets. If you answer any newspaper ads, be cautious! If there are many breeds offered, chances are, it is a small-scale version of a puppy mill. Do not support these individuals by buying from them.

PUPPY MILLS

A puppy farm, or puppy mill, is a place where puppies are mass produced for profit! This is the source for almost all pet stores selling puppies. Puppy mills breed misery. Hundreds of thousands of puppies are raised each year in puppy mills. These mills are distinguished by their cramped, crude, filthy conditions, and the constant breeding of unhealthy and genetically defective dogs, solely for profit.

Female dogs are usually bred the first time they come into heat and are bred every heat cycle. They are bred until their poor worn-out bodies can't reproduce any longer. Then they are killed, either by starvation or shooting them, sold to laboratories or dumped, all because the female is no longer an "effective producer."

Puppies are born on chicken wire, often without shelter from the sun, rain, or snow. Cages are stacked on top of each other, with urine and feces dripping onto the dogs below. Puppies are taken from their mother when they are five to eight weeks old and sold to brokers who pack them into crates for resale to pet stores all over the country. These puppies are shipped by truck or plane and often without adequate food, water, ventilation, or shelter. Almost half of the puppies do not survive the trip. Puppy mills and pet stores maximize their profits by not spending money on proper food, housing, or veterinary care.

The food that is fed in puppy mills is often purchased from dog food companies by the truckload. It is made up of the sweepings from the floor and is so devoid of nutritional value that the dogs' teeth rot at an early age.

Innocent families buy the puppies only to find that the puppy is very ill or has genetic or emotional problems. Often the puppies die of disease. Many others have medical problems that cost thousands of dollars in vet bills. And many have emotional problems because they have not been properly socialized in the mills. Don't bring this misery into your home.

Hearts United for Animals (HUA) has a lot of suggestions on their web site under the Prisoners of Greed. Look under "What You Can Do?" (www.hua.org).

Research from HUA shows that 98% of the puppies sold in pet stores come from facilities that they consider puppy mills. Pet stores will often tell prospective customers that their puppies come from local breeders or quality breeders. Don't believe them, ask to see the paperwork and find out where the puppies really come from.

There are seven states known as puppy mill states because they have the majority of the puppy mills in the country. They are: Missouri, Nebraska, Kansas, Iowa, Arkansas, Oklahoma and Pennsylvania. It is estimated that the puppy industry in Missouri is valued at 40 million dollars a year. The puppy industry in one county in Pennsylvania, Lancaster, is valued at four million dollars a year.

There is a federal law, the Animal Welfare Act, and many states have laws that purport to regulate puppy mills, but the fact is that those laws are rarely enforced. **There is no excuse for these abusive puppy mills to continue.**

The Author

Dr. Marilyn Cochran Mosley is an educational psychologist and has worked with children since 1973. Prior to that she was a counselor at the college level. Most recently she has traveled throughout Alaska as an itinerant school psychologist.

Marilyn was born in Oregon and grew up in the Pacific Northwest. She holds an undergraduate degree in Sociology, and two masters degrees in both Philosophy and Educational Psychology/Counseling. She went on to receive her doctorate degree in Educational Leadership from Seattle University. Marilyn and her two dachshunds live on Vashon Island, along with two griffon pointer mixes and three cats.

Outside her work, Marilyn is an avid photographer, enjoys animals, and loves the outdoors. She also is a gourmet cook, a certified scuba diver, and has held a private pilot's license. Her first book, *Dachshund Tails North*, tells about flying experiences 13,000 miles over Alaska that she and her husband shared with their dachshund crew. *Dachshund Tails Up The Inside Passage*, the sequel, is about the same three fun-loving dachshunds sailing up the Inside Passage to southeastern Alaska. The third book, *Dachshund Tails Down The Yukon*, follows seven dachshunds bent upon mischief as they travel down the Yukon River through Canada's wilderness in a 17-foot canoe.

The Cover's Artist

Sueellen Ross has been a professional artist for 22 years. She currently lives in Seattle with her husband, a black lab and two cats.

ISBN 1553955562-5

9 781553 955627